Murder by Arrangement

by

Suzanne Young

Sybown Press

Cover Designer: Karen Phillips

All rights reserved

Names, characters and incidents depicted in this book are purely fictitious and the products of the author's imagination. The author has also taken the liberty of placing fabricated homes in the middle of actual neighborhoods. Any resemblance to actual persons or places is coincidental and unintentional. Places of interest and historic references are real.

Sybown Press
9028 West 50th Lane, #1
Arvada, CO 80002-4441

This book is dedicated
to Diony and to Bill
with my love.

Other books in the Edna Davies series

Murder by Yew, 2009
Murder by Proxy, 2011
Murder by Mishap, 2012
Murder by Christmas, 2013

Chapter 1

"What do you suppose has upset Irene?" Edna Davies stroked Benjamin's ginger fur as she spoke the thought aloud. One thing about having a cat, he made an excellent confidante and knew how to keep a secret.

This early February morning, she had finally finished addressing valentines to everyone on her Christmas list. Tending to Albert, recovering from an injury, had prevented her from sending yuletide greetings to friends and family at year's end. "I hope hearts are as welcome as holly for those who hear from us only once a year," she had said to Benjamin as she applied the last self-stick postage stamp. She had then invited the cat onto her lap just as the telephone rang.

"I'm glad to catch you at home," Irene said. "If you'll be in today, would you mind if I drive down to talk to you? It's about a family matter."

She sounded untypically serious, so Edna answered immediately, "I'm off to the post office this morning, but I'll be here for the rest of the day. Why don't you come for lunch? The forecast is for snow again, but not until later this afternoon."

After hanging up, she sat stroking Benjamin's back for a few minutes as she tried to imagine what might be so worrisome that her daughter-in-law would make the forty-minute drive from Warwick to South County on such a cold and dismal day. Giving up the mental exercise as fruitless, she turned her thoughts to planning a lunch menu.

Since she and Irene were both perpetually trying to lose an extra ten pounds, Edna decided to make carrot soup and serve it with homemade soda crackers. She'd warm some applesauce and put out one cinnamon sugar cookie each for dessert. Diet or no, they needed a little sugar to balance the meal.

Irene arrived shortly before noon. At five and a half feet, she was an inch taller than Edna with a pleasant round face and ready smile. This daughter-in-law was married to Edna and Albert's eldest child Matthew. Edna found it hard to believe that Matthew and Irene's first born, Joseph, would graduate from high school in another few months. David, their second child, was two years younger, followed by twelve-year-old Allison and nine-year-old Amanda. Edna always smiled with pleasure whenever she thought of the energetic and enthusiastic brood, feeling with some pride that it spoke well of the parents.

"Brrr," said Irene, stepping into the front hall. "I'm ready for spring."

"Are you regretting that you didn't go to Florida with Matthew and Albert?" Edna asked.

"Maybe only because of the sunshine, but I'm no fisherman. No sea legs, I'm afraid." Irene grimaced as she removed her coat, hat and gloves and set them on a nearby chair.

"Me either," Edna said as she thought with dread that she would also have had to board an airplane, had she accepted the half-hearted invitation to join "the boys" on their fishing trip to Miami--"the boys" being her husband Albert, son Matthew, son-in-law Roger and Roger's father Ken Marlstone. They had flown south for a week of fishing with Roger's brother, Patrick, who captained his own trawler. Patrick had recently acquired a second boat for his local business and invited the family on its maiden voyage.

The trip had the added advantage of Florida's sunny weather where Albert could exercise his leg without fear of slipping on ice or being housebound by yet another snowstorm. He still hadn't fully recovered from having fractured his kneecap shortly before Thanksgiving. This accident was why Edna was sending valentines in place of the Christmas cards she'd had no time to write in December.

"Besides, I really couldn't leave with Amanda being off this coming week." Irene's voice broke into Edna's wandering thoughts and recaptured her attention. "I don't know why the schools can't all plan spring break for the same time. Joseph, David and Allison's is the week *after* Amanda's. With a nine-year-old hanging around the house all day, I couldn't ask my mother to come and stay while I went off to play on the beach." Irene's smile slipped when she added, "I'm afraid Mother's showing her age lately. I think she no longer has the energy--or the patience--to put up with four children for a week, even if they are self-sufficient."

Detecting a catch in Irene's throat, Edna reached over to gently squeeze her forearm. "I know it has to be hard for you, dear. I'm here to help whenever you need me." As the younger woman's eyes misted, Edna thought a change of subject would be wise. She didn't want to dwell on a topic that neither one of them could control and which was bound to reduce Irene to tears. "Albert phoned last night to say they had an uneventful flight and were settling into the condo. He and Matthew have a couple of side bets going as to who will catch the first fish and the biggest fish."

That made Irene laugh as she used her fingertips to swipe beneath her eyes. "Yes, Matt called us, too. Joseph and David wanted so badly to go along, but I put my foot down about them missing school. It's a shame Patrick couldn't have rescheduled for week after next, but he'd already booked a sizeable group for those dates." After hanging her coat in the closet, she turned to follow Edna into the kitchen, saying as she did so, "All that aside, I might have caved in and gone if Diane had been able to. It's probably a good thing she's working next week."

Edna chuckled at the thought of her second oldest child, a registered nurse who worked part time for a home health care provider. "She phoned Tuesday evening while Roger was packing. She confessed to being sorely tempted to accept her brother-in-law's invitation and probably would have quit her job, if you had agreed to the trip. It's hard to pass up a vacation south when we've had such a cold and snowy winter."

The two women continued to chat amiably while Edna arranged crackers on a plate and Irene ladled soup into bowls and placed them on the kitchen table. As they ate, Irene brought Edna up to date on the activities of her children. When they were nearly finished with the soup, she came to her youngest, but hesitated as if she didn't know what to say.

"What is it, dear," Edna prompted. "You said on the phone this morning that you wanted to discuss something. Does it have to do with Amanda?"

Irene pushed the remains of her soup around the bottom of the bowl with her spoon. She was quiet for so long that Edna was about to speak again when Irene looked up with worried eyes and nodded. "She has a new best friend. A girl who moved into the neighborhood last month and is in Amanda's third-grade class."

"You don't approve of this new friendship?" Edna guessed.

"It's not that. Not exactly. Violet--or Lettie, as she's called--is a nice girl, extremely well-mannered. If anything, she might be almost too quiet for a nine-year-old." Irene paused, then took a deep breath. "It's her family situation that has me spooked."

"Spooked?" Edna wondered at Irene's choice of word. "How so?"

Irene sat forward, suddenly animated. "Do you remember that scandal a couple years ago? It was all over the news … that financial advisor who was found dead in his townhouse. It happened right here in South County." She kept adding details as if to jog Edna's memory. "Heart failure, but questionable circumstances. You don't remember?"

Edna frowned, trying to recall, but finally shook her head. "It's not sounding familiar."

"It was about two or two and a half years ago."

"No, dear, I don't remember. That was around the time Albert retired and we were exploring the east coast to see where we might want to live, before we found this place."

Irene's face fell, apparently disappointed that Edna hadn't known about the story. "That's right. You were gone for a good part of the year." She sighed, seeming resigned to filling Edna in on some background. "The man's name was Gregory Haverstrum. He was found dead in his townhouse. They said it was cardiac arrest, but rumor was that he had been poisoned."

Edna's interest was piqued, but she thought Irene might be straying from the subject. "And this has something to do with Amanda?"

Irene pushed her plate aside and rested her forearms on the table, leaning forward and lowering her voice as if imparting a secret. "Amanda's new friend is Gregory Haverstrum's daughter. His wife was Rose Haverstrum, but she took back her maiden name. Beck. She goes by Rose Beck now, or actually, she prefers to be called Rosie."

A memory that had been nagging at Edna's subconscious suddenly came into focus. "I think I remember my friend Tuck mentioning this. There was quite a sensation because Rose … ah, Rosie … is from a prominent family. Her mother, Lily Beck, is a member of Greenthumbs, our local garden club." Edna paused, then frowned. "I don't recall Tuck saying anything about poison, though."

Irene looked down briefly at her folded hands before lifting her eyes to Edna's again. "I guess nothing was ever proven, and nobody was arrested, but Rosie was questioned repeatedly over a period of several months. She and her husband had separated about a month before it happened. That's why he was living in a townhouse and was alone when he died. It was a couple of days before he was found."

"She was questioned but never charged with anything?"

Irene shrugged. "Suspicion surrounded his death, but nothing was really clear from the news reports. There was some mention of burns around his mouth, but nobody ever determined if they were relevant to the cause of death or just some sort of medical condition associated with his illness. At the time, Rosie was working in one of the local greenhouses and had access to any number of toxic substances. Not just plants, but pesticides, too. That might've been why they thought she could have put something in his food, but investigators couldn't prove anything. She was called in and questioned over and over, but she was never charged with murdering her husband. Unfortunately for her, nothing was found to build a case for suicide either."

"And Rosie Beck is your new neighbor?"

Irene nodded. "She moved into our neighborhood right after Christmas, one street over."

Edna tried to remember what she'd heard of Lily Beck's family. "Rosie wasn't living in South County before that, was she?"

Irene shook her head. "She sold their house down here and his condo and moved to East Providence after his funeral. Now, she's moved again and in the middle of the school year. That's hard on a child."

Edna said, "How do you know all this? Have you talked with her?"

Irene waggled a hand. "Sort of. Lettie came to

Amanda's birthday party last month. Rosie brought her over so she could meet us. Very properly. I would have done the same. You know, we being strangers and all. Since then, I spoke to her once at the grocery store, and again at the school's parents' night last week. You know, just sort of brief 'how-do's.'" Irene's eyes widened. "I kept thinking she looked familiar but the name threw me. It kept bugging me, so I searched for her on the Internet. I would have remembered about the scandal right away if she was still going by Haverstrum."

Irene sat silently for a moment, frowning at the table top as if organizing her thoughts. Eventually, she began to speak again, slowly at first, as she lifted her head to look at Edna. "Last night, she phoned to invite Amanda to spend some time with Lettie at her grandmother's. I knew from rereading the online reports that Rosie's mother lived near here, so I told Rosie I'd let her know tonight. I wanted to talk to you first, since I thought you might know the mother. I can't wait until Matt comes home to give Rosie an answer, and, besides, it would be hard to explain my feelings to him over the phone, long distance." She sighed. "I thought, if you knew Lily Beck, you could give me your opinion of the family and this whole scandal. Am I being unreasonable if I discourage Amanda's friendship with Lettie?"

Edna brought an image of the older Mrs. Beck to mind. "As I said, Rosie's mother and I belong to the same garden club, so I have met her, but I haven't spent a lot of time in her company. She's pretty reclusive. Doesn't have much to do with anyone except an occasional meeting with members of Greenthumbs. She has one of the best gardens in the area and can't help showing it off. I was among the lucky ones to be selected last month to view some of her winter blooms. I took pictures and thought I'd sketch either her Christmas Rose or the Lily of the Valley bush as a 'thank you' present." When Edna noticed that she was losing Irene's attention, she hesitated. "But you don't want to know about my garden club, I'm sure. What exactly do you wish to know?"

"To be frank, Edna, I wonder if Rosie *did* kill her husband. You know what they say about no smoke without fire."

"Oh, my." The bluntness of Irene's statement startled Edna. She thought back to when they'd just moved to southern Rhode Island and she'd been suspected of poisoning her handyman. She remembered how upset and humiliated she'd been to realize her new neighbors and friends dared not eat anything she prepared. Many even refused to come to her house. Silent rejection is hard to fight. "Do *you* think you're being unfair? After all, she was never charged with anything, and you said yourself that poison was only a rumor."

"I'd rather be accused of unfairness than have anything happen to one of my children. How could I live with myself if I exposed Amanda to a murderer?"

Edna considered her daughter-in-law's concern. "But what if Rosie is innocent? Gossip and innuendos can be very destructive."

Irene shrugged and lowered her head, not meeting Edna's eyes. "I suppose so."

Edna persisted. "Why would she want to kill her

husband?"

"The talk was that he'd had more than one affair. As a matter of fact, one of his latest was a woman who worked with Rosie and, supposedly, was her best friend." Irene made a weak attempt to lighten the mood. "Husbands have been killed for less, if you watch the soap operas."

Edna appreciated the humor, but shook her head in dismay. "Sounds like Gregory Haverstrum wasn't a nice man, but surely infidelity isn't a sufficient enough reason for murder."

"Perhaps not," agreed Irene. "If it were, I think the girlfriend might have been killed, too." She scowled. "I don't understand how someone can work alongside her best friend, day in and day out, while carrying on with that friend's husband. I can easily imagine Rosie being angry enough to murder that backstabber."

Listening to her daughter-in-law's rant with only half an ear, Edna's mind jumped back to her early days in the community, and she felt again the despair of her own situation when she'd been confronted with the murder of her handyman. Then, she thought of her granddaughter for a moment. Would she be subjecting Amanda to possible harm if she were to side with Rosie, or should she agree with Irene who, Edna now suspected, had come looking for support, not argument?

I should meet Rosie before I decide how to answer Irene, Edna thought, as an idea began to form in her mind. "You said you would let Rosie know your answer by this evening?"

"That's right. Tomorrow's Friday, so the girls will be in school until mid-afternoon. Rosie wants to bring them down here as soon after that as possible. She works for an event planner now. This is one of their busiest times of the year with all the Valentine's Day weddings. She'll be working long hours next week, which is why Lettie will stay with her Grandmother Lily for the school break. I think Rosie feels that Lettie will be happier if she has a friend with her, even if it's only for part of the time."

Edna stood to clear the soup bowls from the table and get their dessert. After a couple of minutes of silence while she worked through the plan in her head, she said. "How would it be if Amanda spent a few days with me?"

Irene looked a bit startled at the suggestion, then thoughtful. "I suppose …" she began.

Edna rushed on, explaining her idea. "I'd like to meet Rosie, get a feel for the sort of person she is. Why don't you invite her to lunch at your house tomorrow? Tell her I've asked Amanda to stay with me for a few nights, so I'll be there for lunch, as well." Edna paused, thinking, then added, "It will be a good chance for her to meet me, too. The girls will be able to see each other, and the question of an overnight needn't arise. Besides, it would be a treat for me to visit with my granddaughter. It's rare that I see her without the rest of the family around."

Irene narrowed her eyes, but couldn't help grinning. She'd been married to Matthew long enough to have gotten to know her mother-in-law fairly well. "What are you up to, Edna? I detect a glimmer in your eye."

Edna felt a sudden surge of anticipation in talking to a woman who had been in a similar situation as she.

Evasively, she said, "After lunch, I could save Rosie a trip by driving both girls down and dropping Lettie off at her grandmother's. Kill two birds with one stone, so to speak."

Chapter 2

"Watcha doin'?" Mary's voice came from the mudroom as she appeared in the doorway to the kitchen.

Irene had gone home shortly after lunch, leaving Edna to wash up. Now lost in thought, she nearly dropped the saucepan she'd been drying while gazing out the kitchen window at clouds the color of a gray cat's fur. *Mary's forever startling me since she's become used to walking in unannounced. Maybe I'll install a doorbell in the back door, so she can signal her arrival,* Edna mused wryly, taking a deep breath. Nerves steadied, she turned to welcome her friend, but what she saw startled her.

She had always thought Mary might be considered plain but for her brilliant green eyes. Today, those eyes had dark circles beneath them. Her curly, carroty-red hair looked as if it had been brushed hurriedly before being gathered at the nape of her neck with a white Scrunchie.

Edna held out a hand, palm up, toward one of the kitchen chairs. "Sit and have some tea. It'll take me only a minute to make a fresh pot."

"Okay."

Edna had inherited Mary Osbourne as her nearest neighbor when she and Albert moved into their dream retirement home next door to the lanky redhead. After

Albert retired, selling his share of a medical practice in Providence, he and Edna had spent a year driving from Rhode Island to South Carolina and back, looking for an ideal place to pass their "golden years." Eventually, they decided to move no farther than South County in their own home state. The area had everything they enjoyed, from beaches to farms and woodlands. The state university's main Kingston campus was close by for lectures, plays and concerts; and Providence was only an hour's drive when they wanted to enjoy the wealth of social and cultural activities in the "big city." Along with the Davieses' cozy Cape Cod cottage came several garden plots, hand-written and illustrated journals of the myriad plantings by the former owner Hazel Rabichek, and a quirky and snoopy but concerned neighbor.

Dressed this afternoon in her winter camouflage outfit with its design of pine needles and bare branches on a white background, Mary was a true free spirit. She'd been raised mostly by a spinster cousin after Mary's birth had both surprised and baffled her parents just when they'd settled nicely into their childless forties. A willful and curious child, Mary had set the previously sedate household on its ear. Now, in her mid-fifties, she lived alone in the family's three-story mansion--alone, that is, except for a dog and four cats.

Sagging onto a chair next to the one occupied by Benjamin, Mary stroked his golden coat while she waited for Edna to pour the tea and set out a plate of cranberry muffins, warm from the oven. Uncharacteristically, she was silent until Edna took the seat on the opposite side of the table. When she still hadn't said a word, Edna prompted. "What's wrong,

Mary. You look tired."

"Haven't been sleeping," Mary said, picking up her mug and taking a cautious sip of the steaming liquid.

"Why not? Are you ill?"

The redhead shook her head. "'S not that. It's the ghost in my attic."

Edna nearly choked on the tea she'd just sipped. Seeing the forlorn look on Mary's face, she bit back a laugh and said as calmly as she could, "you have a ghost in your attic?"

Mary nodded.

"What makes you say that?"

"Noises at night. Keeps me awake."

Edna thought for a moment while she broke off a piece of muffin. After chewing and swallowing, she decided to play along, wondering if Mary were joking or hallucinating. She definitely was acting odd this morning, even for her. "Is this a sudden phenomenon?" Edna asked. "I know your house is old and probably has quite a history, but I haven't heard you mention the possibility of it being haunted before."

"Just started up a week ago. Never heard 'im before." Mary was studying Edna's face as if judging her reaction. "Now, I hear 'im every night."

"Hmmm," Edna murmured. "Do you believe in ghosts?"

Mary shrugged as she reached for a muffin. "I dunno. Never thought about it one way or the other, but I've never heard noises like these before. Can't think what else could cause such a racket."

"Have you gone upstairs to check?"

Mary shook her head vehemently, her mouth full

again. Swallowing quickly, she blurted. "No way. I'm not goin' up there alone."

"Could it be the pipes? Time-worn houses develop strange noises, particularly with steam heat clanging away in those ancient radiators."

Mary shook her head again. "Nope. I know all the sounds that house makes. This is new. Upstairs. Comin' from my old nursery."

"What about squirrels or raccoons? They're notorious for getting into people's attics."

"I've been up there in the daylight. There're no signs of the sort left by squirrels or mice or any other wild animal, but things have been knocked over. So you see, *something*'s gotta have done that. Things don't just fall over by themselves."

Edna didn't know how to respond to that bit of information. "What does Hank do?" She asked instead about the black Labrador Mary had inherited after his owner died. "Most dogs would bark or whine or whimper, I imagine."

"Nothing. Sometimes, if he wakes up, he stands up, turns around and plops back down to sleep again."

"I'm surprised you haven't gone up to explore."

"Not me. No way. I'm no ghost buster. Not by myself. Not in the dark."

"How are you going to find out what's causing the ruckus, if you don't go look?"

"I thought you'd come stay with me and we could investigate together." Mary narrowed her eyes and stared at Edna for a few seconds, as if deciding whether or not to say something else. Edna had raised her cup halfway to her mouth when Mary announced, almost proudly, "Actually, I think I know who it is."

Edna, glad she didn't have hot tea in her mouth this time, carefully lowered the cup back onto its saucer. "Oh?"

"Yup," Mary dipped her chin in a firm nod. "He's a rebel."

Edna kept a straight face, so as not to hurt her neighbor's feelings. She could see that Mary was perfectly serious. "A rebel," Edna repeated.

"Has to be," Mary said. "I've been thinking a lot about it and remembered something my father told me when I was little."

Knowing her neighbor liked to be prompted, Edna said, "And what was that?"

"He told me that the main part of our house was built in the early seventeen hundreds, before the Revolutionary War." Maddeningly, she stopped talking to take a bite of muffin and a sip of tea.

"And …" Edna encouraged.

"Did you know Rhode Island was the first of the British colonies to declare independence in seventeen seventy-six?"

"No," Edna admitted, "but what does that have to do with a rebel haunting your old nursery." She thought her comment might make Mary smile at the very least, but her neighbor went on with a serious expression.

"I've been rereading my history books about what went on in this area at that time and remembered the Gaspee Affair."

It was Edna's turn to nod. "When Rhode Island traders attacked a British customs ship. But that took place off Gaspee Point in Warwick, didn't it?"

"That's right. It was a few years before the Revolution, but people around here didn't like the British ships patrolling Narragansett Bay to stop 'em from trading. When war really started, the English raided farms on this side and then retreated over to Newport because the colonists over there were Loyalists. Not us on this side of the Bay. Our guys fought back. Plenty of skirmishes started by the local farmers and fishermen."

"Okay," Edna said, "but what does that have to do with noises in your attic?"

"I'm coming to that," Mary said. "The original owner of my house was a physician, so I figure maybe, if one of the rebels was wounded, he might have sought medical help. The doctor could have hidden him upstairs. The top floor was servants quarters, originally. It wasn't a nursery until my father had the inside walls knocked down to make two big rooms. One's the nursery and the other's storage space."

"So you think the rebel might have died from his wounds and now his ghost is roaming around?"

Mary nodded, studying Edna's face as to assure herself that Edna was taking her seriously.

"Why do you think he decided to appear now? Why not years ago?"

"Dunno," Mary said, sounding dejected and then defensive. "Can't explain it. All I know is there's somethin' going on over my head at night."

Edna didn't want to antagonize Mary, so she posed another question. "Do you think a window shutter or a roof shingle could be loose? The wind has been pretty strong the last few nights."

Mary shook her head. "That's not the sort of noise I'm hearing." She pushed her mug aside and slumped back in her chair. "It's coming from inside. He's in the nursery."

"What else could it be then?" Edna said, truly curious and purposely avoiding Mary's last pronouncement. "You said Hank's asleep. What about the cats? Do the noises disturb them too?"

"Spot doesn't wake up." Mary said, mentioning her year-old black cat who had come to her as a stray. She sat forward and seemed to be thinking aloud. "I get ready for bed and shut Auntie Bea, Charcoal and Snowball in Father's old room before I watch the late-night news. There's a bathroom off the bedroom for their litter box, and I put water in the sink for them to drink. Father's room is the best place. I don't have to worry about them getting into stuff or getting hurt while I'm asleep."

Edna thought of the three felines Mary had adopted after the woman who owned them had been killed shortly before Christmas. Two of them, one pure white and the other all black, were about eight months old. Auntie Bea was an older Maine Coon who seemed to chaperone the youngsters. "Why don't you keep them in your room?"

Mary frowned as if the question were absurd. "I'm finally used to Spot and Hank sleeping with me," she said. "The two kittens are full of energy and pretty playful, so they're probably up half the night. I'd never get any sleep if they were all in my room."

Edna didn't bother to point out that Mary wasn't getting any sleep with a ghost wandering around, either.

Instead, she said, "Speaking of Hank and Spot, where are they?" She'd been so distracted by Mary's revelation that she hadn't noticed her neighbor's nearly constant companions were missing. They almost always accompanied her when she came to visit. Both dog and cat enjoyed saying hello to Benjamin.

"Left them home. Gotta go to work soon. I just came by to ask you a favor."

"I thought you were switching to a lunchtime shift at the hospital," Edna said, glancing up at the kitchen clock on the wall.

Mary shook her head. "Nope. Thought about it, but the nurses told me they have trouble getting volunteers for the dinner hour." She shrugged. "I work only three days a week, and I'm used to starting at four o'clock. Hank and Spot are used to that schedule, too. When I get home, we go for a walk. Then, they settle down for the night."

Wondering about Mary's other pets, Edna said, "When will you let the new cats out of the house? Don't you think they've gotten used to their surroundings by now? I wouldn't think they'd get lost or run away, after living with you for the past six or seven weeks."

Mary slumped back in her chair again. "I'm not gonna let 'em out, not with Snowball being deaf. I'd be afraid she'd get run over or grabbed by a fox or something." She reached over to stroke Benjamin. "As far as I know, they've always been house cats, so they'll be fine."

An image of Snowball, the pure white kitten, came into Edna's mind. She had learned it was the gene for the cat's pretty blue eyes that also caused her deafness.

Charcoal, her black companion, was good about sticking close to her. The two were rarely out of each other's sight. Auntie Bea, the older Maine Coon, also seemed to be conscious of the kitten's handicap and didn't stray far from the frolicking pair.

Thinking of Mary's most recent adoptees, Edna said, "Could it be the cats who are making noise at night?"

Mary shook her head. "They're at the other end of the house. The sounds're above me, in the nursery. Sorta like someone stomping or running."

Edna decided to distract her neighbor from further discussion of the ghost. "You came over to ask me a favor?"

At that moment, Mary turned to look up at the wall clock. "Oops. Speaking of which … I gotta get to the hospital. I'll be home a little after eight tonight. Since Al's out of town, can you come stay over?"

"Albert," Edna corrected automatically before shaking her head. Briefly explaining she'd be having lunch with Irene the next day and bringing two girls back afterwards, she concluded by saying, "And before I head for my daughter-in-law's in Warwick, I have my weekly hair appointment. I don't want to be up all night before a very busy day tomorrow."

Instead of looking disappointed, as Edna had expected, Mary perked up. "That's great. Your grandkids are really good with Hank and the cats. Amanda and her friend can come over with you tomorrow night. We can hunt for the ghost together. They'll love it."

"Hold on," Edna said, thinking Mary's scheme

would turn out to be a wild-goose chase and lead only to two tired and possibly cranky girls on Saturday. "I'm not promising anything. We'll wait and see. At the very least, I'll have to get permission from the friend's grandmother."

As usual, Mary wasn't the least deterred, not with the possibility of children helping out. Ignoring Edna's words, she smiled and stood abruptly, "I really gotta go. I'll call ya later." With those words, she headed toward the mudroom and the back door.

It was only when Mary had gone that Edna thought she should have asked her about the Haverstrum scandal. Of course, she'd be the one to ask. Mary always knew more than anyone else about the comings and goings around town. Edna mentally kicked herself for not thinking of it sooner, but she *had* been a little distracted by Mary's ghost story.

Chapter 3

Early the following morning, Edna left for her hair appointment shortly after Bev and Junie showed up. Not only were Fridays the day Housekeeper Helpers cleaned her house, but it was also her "coiffure and cuisine" morning with her friends Helen Tucker and Harriet Peppafitch, known to most who knew them as Tuck and Peppa.

First, the three women met at The Locks Shoppe in town. Typically, this meant a trim for Edna and Peppa, both of whom kept their gray curls short. Since the root touchup on Tuck's blonde hair took a while before the thick tresses were swept back into a French twist, Edna and Peppa waited for her in a nearby café. Over brunch, a week's worth of gossip and personal news kept them at their usual table until the lunch crowd began to arrive, at which time the "coiff 'n cuis" members went their separate ways.

Edna had known Tuck since college days when she'd married one of Albert's fraternity brothers from the nearby state university. The Tuckers had remained in the Kingston area while the Davieses moved to Providence, but the two couples had kept in close contact over the years.

"Look no more," Tuck's husband, a realtor, said when Edna and Albert had begun to doubt their ideal house existed at all. "I've got the perfect place for you, and it's only a stone's throw from Tuck and me."

Sadly, he died of a heart attack two weeks before the closing. Needing a distraction from her bereavement, Tuck had taken it upon herself to introduce Edna to the community by way of the garden club and social events at the nearby university. At the same time, Harriet Peppafitch had been fervently working to distract Tuck from her grief by getting her involved in library funding and scholarship committees, two activities of interest to Edna. Inevitably, Edna and Peppa met and became friends, nearly as close to each other as they were to Tuck.

Peppa, one of the mainstays of the local town, had recently retired after heading the library for nearly forty years. She was known by everyone who grew up in the region as the Saturday morning story lady. Her hour-long readings had been divided between preschoolers for the first thirty minutes and older children for the last half hour. She'd finally stepped down when budget cuts threatened the job of her second-in-command, a forty-five year old woman who wasn't as prepared to retire as Peppa. Now, for a few hours a week, the former librarian kept her hand in and her eye on the place as a volunteer.

Edna looked forward to her Friday socializing, so it was with regret that she had to leave that morning in the middle of Tuck's report on the latest antics of her three-year-old great-granddaughter.

Merging onto Route 1 and heading north to Warwick, Edna's thoughts turned to her own family and stopped to dwell on her youngest child. Starling would be thirty-one in April. She'd been dating a local police detective for over a year, but only since Christmas, after returning from a week's skiing trip to Colorado, had she seemed more attentive to Charlie Rogers. Idly, Edna speculated whether or not they might announce their engagement on Valentine's Day.

Edna first met the detective when Tuck had been the victim of a gang of antique thieves. Within a day of that crime, Charlie was interrogating Edna as the prime suspect in the murder of her handyman. Stumbling over one another during both those investigations, Edna and the policeman had developed a mutual respect that had grown stronger through another couple of mishaps in the last year. Despite their rocky beginnings, she was very fond of Charlie and thought he'd make a fine addition to the family.

Maybe Valentine's Day when her father is back from Florida next week, Edna thought and, since it was out of her control, pushed the idea to the back of her mind as she drew closer to Irene and Matthew's house. Turning onto their street, she began to wonder what sort of woman her son's newest neighbor would be. Was she an innocent victim or a shrewd killer?

As Edna pulled into the driveway and got out of the car, a blonde woman was mounting the two steps to the front door. Even if Rose hadn't been carrying a small pink suitcase, Edna would have recognized her. The previous evening, Edna had skimmed through some of the online news about the Haverstrum scandal. Included in the reports had been several photos of the dead man's wife, so Edna immediately recognized the woman. Rose *Beck*, Edna reminded herself that the woman had resumed her maiden name. Her hair was longer, worn straight and pulled back into a loose ponytail instead of stylishly curled as in her old photographs, but she was still beautiful enough to turn heads. She huddled into a black, thigh-length woolen coat against the day's chill, and focused large blue eyes on Edna as she approached.

"You must be Rose." Edna removed a glove and held out her hand.

The woman's grip was firm and cool as she greeted Edna with a gentle smile. "Rosie, please," she said, then wrinkled her nose as if momentarily smelling something sour. "Mother's the only one who calls me Rose. Besides that, I thought it sounded too pretentious when I started working in a greenhouse, and I wanted to avoid any confusion as to whether someone wanted to order the flower or speak to the florist." She gave a short laugh and her expression returned to one of pleasure. "You must be Irene's mother-in-law."

As if hearing her name, the hostess herself opened the door, preventing any awkwardness that might have ensued had the two strangers been kept on the stoop for long. "I thought I heard someone at the door. Come in. The girls won't be home from school for a couple of hours yet, so we have lots of time to visit."

Their initial conversation was about the recently unpredictable weather and Irene's prettily decorated table with red roses and white baby's breath. "An early sweetheart present from my husband," Irene said, as she ladled butternut squash soup into blue Peter Pots bowls and passed a platter of mini croissants filled with tuna salad. A comfortable silence, which fell as the women began to eat, was broken only by murmurs of how good the food was. When appetites had been somewhat sated, Rosie addressed Edna.

"It's very kind of you to drive Lettie to her grandmother's. Valentine's Day is one of the busiest times of the year for event planners, as I'm sure you can imagine. With all the weddings we're working on, I didn't know when I could get free to make the trip myself. Lily won't take her car out of the garage if she even *thinks* the weather's going to be bad."

"I'm looking forward to meeting your daughter," Edna replied, ignoring the bitter-sounding comment about Rosie's mother. She concentrated on laying her spoon on the plate beside her soup bowl, wondering how to approach the subject of the husband's death, when Irene spoke up.

"Lettie's such a nice girl. She and Amanda have really hit it off, and in such a short time. You'd think they were soul mates."

Rosie's eyes sparkled with genuine pleasure for the first time since they'd sat down. "Yes. Lettie's grades have already improved. She seems happy at her new school." Growing more serious, she said, "Her friendship with Amanda has a lot to do with it."

Edna recognized an opportunity. "Has she been very unhappy?"

When Rosie turned to Edna, anger flickered in her eyes for an instant before she lowered her lids and looked down at the twisted napkin in her hands. She took a slow breath before lifting her head. "My daughter has been sweet and cheerful since the day she was born." Pausing for a moment, Rosie studied Edna's face first and then Irene's. Taking another deep breath, she gave a curt nod as if making up her mind to something.

"Look. I realize you know who I am, and I'm pretty sure you read at the time, or at least heard rumors that I was a suspect when my husband died. Two years ago, I moved to East Providence to get away from the distrust and suspicion on everyone's face. I figured a new community would mean a clean start, but the neighbors soon found out who I was and it started again. People either glaring or turning away so they didn't have to look at me." Her voice grew stronger as her anger quickened. "I thought I could take it. I thought everyone was being cruel only to me, but Lettie began to notice. She's so young and innocent. She doesn't understand." Rosie's voice faltered when she added more quietly, "Then I learned she was being taunted and bullied by the kids in school, and my heart broke." Rosie bent her head again, but not before Edna saw the wetness in her eyes.

She thought Rosie could use a moment to recover and might also like to know that she wasn't alone in that sort of treatment. "May I tell you about my move to South County? It was probably around the time you left the area."

Rosie dabbed at her eyes with a crumpled napkin before looking up. Her brow wrinkled as if she were wondering what Edna's move had to do with her difficulties, but she merely nodded.

Edna glanced quickly toward her daughter-in-law. She'd never spoken of her misadventure to anyone in the family except Starling who had played a part in the drama. She wondered what Irene would make of the story. Giving a mental shrug, she decided she'd deal with the family fallout later. At the moment, she thought only of bringing some comfort to Rosie Beck. "Two months after Albert and I moved into the retirement home of our dreams, I was suspected of poisoning our handyman."

If her words were meant to shock, they succeeded. Not only did Rosie's eyes grow wide, but Edna heard a sharp intake of breath from Irene's direction.

"Oh, my goodness," Irene said, raising both hands to her cheeks in surprise. "I never heard about this. Does Matt know?"

Edna shook her head. "I didn't want the rest of the family to worry. It's in the past. Will you keep this our secret?"

Irene reached over and gently squeezed Edna's wrist. "Of course. I'm so sorry I didn't know at the time. If nothing else, I would have offered you my shoulder to lean on." In her usual fashion, Irene attempted a light mood.

Appreciating her daughter-in-law's support, Edna smiled and patted her hand. "I've always been able to count on you, dear. If events had gotten more serious, I would certainly have called you."

Irene settled back, but kept a cautious eye on Edna's face, as if uncertain what to expect after this initial jolt.

Edna took a deep breath as she tried to decide where to begin. She realized at once how difficult it was going to be to relive the experience, not only for what she'd gone through, but also because she'd lost a good friend. For several seconds she thought of Tom Greene and felt again the stress of those seemingly endless days during which she'd been certain she'd be charged with murder and thrown in jail.

"What happened?" Rosie's question, with curiosity, anxiety and impatience all rolled into those two words, made Edna realize that she'd drifted back in time while the other two women were waiting intently for her to explain.

She gave them an edited version of how her handyman had been rushed to the hospital in a coma from which he never emerged. The taxine in his system came from the yew bush, two of which Edna had been pruning the day her handyman died. He'd last been known to visit Edna where he'd had tea and cookies, both containing ingredients out of her herb garden.

"I'll never forget the feeling of isolation when my new friends and neighbors made up all sorts of excuses to avoid coming to my home. If they did visit, they refused to eat or drink anything and left as soon as politely possible. I don't know what was worse, the police questioning me or the silent accusations of everyone around me."

Rosie's head nodded in slow agreement with Edna's description of the helplessness she'd felt. Sudden tears filled her eyes and threatened to spill over. "I know," she said in an unsteady voice. "It isn't fair. I was never arrested." She emitted an unsteady sigh. "There are times I wish they *had* charged me."

"Oh, no, Rosie. Don't ever say that," Edna urged.

"Were *you* arrested?" Irene, still wary, studied Edna's face.

"No, dear. Fortunately, the real killer was caught before it came to that. I had a narrow escape, though." Thinking to offset the startling news for Irene, Edna added, "It's when and how I met Charlie Rogers for the first time."

Before Irene could respond, Rosie spoke. "The police never formally said Gregory didn't commit suicide, so the insurance company refused to pay me his life insurance. They also never said he was murdered, but the reporters all implied it, so it's hanging over my head." She was playing with her spoon and looking at neither Edna nor Irene. It was almost as though she were speaking to herself.

"Is the case still open?" Edna asked.

"It's what they call a 'cold case.' Not officially closed but I don't think anyone's been working on it." Rosie paused before adding, "Until recently, that is. The first detective who questioned me at the time showed up several weeks ago." She sighed as she gazed across at Edna. "I called his department to complain, but they told me he retired last year. Whatever he's doing has nothing to do with them, so I don't know why he's asking questions again." Her mouth twisted in a bitter smile. "I feel like I'm his pet project and he has nothing else to do."

"Maybe he discovered new evidence." Edna had read that there had been at least two other suspects, but she wanted to hear what Rosie had to say. Suddenly realizing how painful the retelling must be for her, Edna hurriedly asked, "Do you mind discussing it?"

Studying Edna's face, Rosie paused as if to consider her answer. Edna was beginning to think the woman would remain silent when she gave a brief nod. "After hearing your story, I think I can talk about what happened to me." Still, she remained silent for a minute, staring at the nearly empty soup bowl in front of her.

When Rosie cleared her throat as if ready to speak, tears again glistened in her eyes, and when her voice cracked, Irene stood abruptly. She bent and put her arms around her neighbor's shoulders, giving her a quick hug. Then, glancing at Edna, she said, "Why don't we take our tea into the living room where we'll be more comfortable."

Realizing her daughter-in-law was giving Rosie time to gain control of her emotions, Edna stood to help gather cups. As she did so, she caught Irene's eye, winked and smiled her approval. In the living room, she sat at the opposite end of a sofa from Rosie and shifted slightly to face the woman. They were seated before a small gas fireplace which Irene turned on to take the winter chill off the room before she settled into a stuffed chair at right angles to both Edna and the hearth.

After taking a slow sip of her tea, Rosie put her cup on the coffee table and sat back to rub her forehead, as if scrubbing away a headache. "It's hard to know where to begin," she said.

"What happened between you two? Why did the police think you might have had something to do with your husband's death?" Edna suggested.

The younger woman's eyes shifted toward Edna, but without focus as if looking into the past. She shrugged. "They asked me what I knew about burns on his mouth. Thought I might have given him something from the nursery I worked in. I guess that, along with our having separated a month before, made them want to blame me." She gave Edna and Irene a crooked smile. "And isn't it always the spouse who's the main suspect?"

"Did you know he was cheating on you?" Irene said, her expression one of disbelief that a wife wouldn't know her husband's actions.

Rosie grimaced. "He was a financial advisor. He often met with clients in the evening. Guess that made it easy for him to get out of the house, and for me to pretend everything was fine between us." She shrugged. "Things hadn't been great with us for months, but when I found out he was having an affair with my *friend*," Rosie nearly spat the word, "I told him to get out. I really figured if he thought he'd lose me, he'd straighten out and we could get back together. We'd be happy again."

"And did he straighten out?" Edna asked when Rosie fell silent.

She shook her head. "I'll never know. A month after he moved out of the house, he was dead."

"Did they ever find out what caused his death?"

"For lack of anything else, the death certificate says heart failure," Rosie said.

Irene's eyes widened. She seemed fascinated by the story, her eyes glued to Rosie's face. "What about the burns you mentioned? Did they ever determine if they were related to how he died?"

When the woman hesitated, Edna answered for her. "I doubt it. I know from listening to Albert that lab technicians have to have some idea of what to look for in order to run conclusive toxicology tests. They don't do a lot of guessing because the tests are expensive. So, unless a symptom or a substance can be identified …"

She stopped when a commotion from the hallway interrupted her and two young girls bounded into the room.

There was no more time to talk about Rosie's situation, and soon the two mothers were waving them off. Edna made certain the girls were securely settled in the back seat before getting into the car. As she opened the driver's door and stopped to lift a hand in farewell, her eyes were drawn to Rosie Beck. The woman was staring intently at the rear window, as if she were about to change her mind and call her daughter back. Without knowing why, Edna felt a sudden shiver of unease.

Chapter 4

Edna glanced into her rear view mirror at the two heads huddled together over the mobile phone in Lettie's hands. Short auburn curls on one girl and long blond locks on the other. Amanda had inherited Edna's coloring and solid build. Lettie was a young version of her thin, graceful mother.

The girls were chattering and giggling, softly at first, but then louder as they forgot about their driver and lost themselves in whatever game they seemed to be playing. Edna smiled, returning her eyes to the road and the Friday afternoon traffic headed south on Interstate 95.

Snow from the night before lay like a thin, white blanket on the dirt-encrusted pack that remained from two previous storms. The afternoon temperature had risen only into the low forties, but Edna was cheered by the sunshine. She let her mind drift back to the conversation with Rosie Beck. Pondering her initial reaction to the woman, Edna thought *Pleasant enough*. She didn't want to think she'd been prejudiced by Rosie's history with the police, not after what Edna herself had suffered. Why then, the uncertainty about the woman?

Edna needed to know more about the husband's death and why the police had concentrated their attentions on his wife. Was it solely because law enforcement personnel always grilled the spouse first?

How am I to find out? Edna wondered only briefly as she realized Mary would almost certainly have information not reported in the news. Edna thought possibly Charlie might also have been involved in the investigation. Those speculations kept her mind busy until she reached her exit off the highway.

She slowed as she approached Lily Beck's yellow bungalow with its wide veranda and dormer windows. The house, Edna had learned from Tuck, had been built in nineteen thirty by Lily's late husband's grandfather. In their early days, bungalows were much larger than their later counterparts, and that was certainly true of this rambling structure. Beyond the house and a patch of side garden, Edna pulled onto the pavement in front of a four-car garage. With a second story above, the building looked nearly as large as the main house.

Before double-wide doors, the driveway was deep enough for two cars to sit bumper to bumper. Edna noticed that someone had neatly shoveled yesterday's snow from the entire paved area. She stopped immediately off the road so as not to crowd the woman standing beside a shiny black, vintage Impala that was parked in front of the second bay. Lily Beck was speaking to a man on the opposite side of the hood. From her gestures, she was apparently pointing out spots he'd missed with his polishing rag which he then dutifully attacked with the cloth in his hand. So intent was she that she didn't turn until Edna's car doors opened and the girls scrambled out.

In her early sixties, Lily was a statuesque woman

with wavy salt-and-pepper hair that hung loose to her shoulders. Wearing a woolen coat that had seen better days, she bent to hug Lettie and smile at Amanda before waving to Edna.

"Hello," she called. "Rose phoned to say you'd be bringing Violet, but I didn't expect you quite so soon. You made good time."

"Yes, we beat the worst of the rush-hour traffic," Edna said and extended a hand, palm up, toward Amanda. "I'd like you to meet my granddaughter Amanda."

Lily solemnly shook the hand the girl offered before speaking in a surprisingly stern tone to Lettie. "Where's your suitcase?"

"In the car," her granddaughter said quietly with a glance at the Buick's back end.

When Edna released the trunk latch with her remote and started toward the rear of the car, Lily barked another order. "Clem will get it," she said, jerking her head toward the lean man standing beside the Impala. "Clem, take Violet's suitcase and leave it inside the front door. No farther. Just inside the door."

As he approached, Edna saw that Clem was older than she'd first thought him to be. Early seventies, she guessed. Although quite thin, he looked physically fit, and his skin was weathered, as if he spent most of his time outdoors. In the stillness following Lily's command, Edna wondered if the man were used to his employer's abruptness. She herself couldn't imagine ordering someone about with such rudeness.

Having obediently picked up the pink luggage, Clem was mounting the steps to the veranda before

Lettie broke the growing silence. "Can I show Amanda my room?" she asked her grandmother in a voice so soft that Edna barely heard her.

Before Lily could respond, Amanda distracted them all. "Gramma, look. You have a flat tire." She was pointing at the Buick's front end.

Hurrying around to her granddaughter's side, Edna's heart sank. While the tire wasn't exactly flat, it had lost enough air that it couldn't possibly get them home. "Drat," she muttered, staring for several seconds, wanting what her eyes saw not to be true. Finally, resignedly, she looked up at Lily. "I'll call the garage and have them send someone out, but I'm afraid I'll have to impose on you until it's fixed. I hope that won't be inconvenient."

"Don't bother calling anyone. Clem will take care of it."

The man who had just been volunteered approached in time to hear. Nodding at Edna, he said, "Probably picked up a nail. If you'll give me your keys, I'll see what I can do." His voice, although raspy, was pleasant and surprisingly cultured. His face was turned away from his employer and, as he reached out a hand, his light blue eyes held a twinkle.

Feeling uncomfortable at Lily's belligerence toward this seemingly kind and gentle man, Edna smiled. "That would be very nice. Thank you," she added, handing him her key ring.

Abruptly, Lily said, "Come have a cup of tea while you wait, Edna. Violet, show Amanda your room, and take your bag upstairs when you go."

The girls ran off, followed more slowly by the

grandmothers. "Workmen. Got to keep an eye on them or they'll take advantage of you," Lily commented, not lowering her voice as she linked her arm in Edna's.

Edna glanced over her shoulder to see Clem pulling tools out of the trunk. Either he hadn't heard or was ignoring Lily. Feeling both gratitude and sympathy for him, Edna said, "How fortunate you are to have a handyman. We've been relying on students from the university. They're good, but what with exams and semester breaks, we can't always count on the same person being available. Seems we're always training someone new."

Lily nodded as she slowly drew Edna along the sidewalk. "Hired him last fall to help with the garden and building repairs. Place has become too big for me to handle alone. I let him use the apartment above the garage, in lieu of wages. He's to paint the house as soon as the weather warms up."

As they crossed the porch to the front door, Edna noticed that, indeed, the house needed not only a good coat or two of paint, but repairs to some of the trim. Unlike the buildings, she knew the gardens to be well-tended and immaculate. The yard was apparently where Lily expended her time and energy. Edna made a mental note to complete the Christmas Rose water color she had in mind for Lily. She had made up her mind to the single white blossom rather than the clustered blooms of the Lily of the Valley bush. The painting was to be a "thank you" for the special invitation and viewing last month. Seeing Lily's January blossoms had been a treat. Although Mrs. Rabichek, the previous owner of the Davies property, had filled her gardens with unusual plants, none bloomed in winter like Lily's.

The women settled in Lily's sun room overlooking the back garden. As soon as they were settled in the comfortable, cushioned wicker chairs, Edna said, "I noticed the abandoned beehive when I was here for your garden tour last month. Was your husband the keeper?"

Lily gazed at the weather-worn hive with its white, peeling paint that stood against the back stone wall and shook her head. "No. It was a few years after his death that I decided to try keeping bees. Thought it would be good for the garden, and I could benefit from the honey." She chuckled. "Best laid plans and all that. When the beekeeper came out that first year, he warned me against the honey. He said, what with all the rhododendron and azaleas around, never mind that Pieris japonica over there next to the hive, the honey would make me sick, more like as not."

Edna knew the Pieris japonica as "Lily of the Valley shrub," but she was getting better at using the botanical names since she'd joined Greenthumbs. The garden club members seemed to prefer the scientific references. "I haven't gotten rid of the old thing because I like the looks of it there. Plugged up the holes, of course, so bees can't get in." Lily's voice broke into Edna's thoughts.

For the next hour, the two women drank tea and chatted about plants and grandchildren. It was a lovely, sun-warmed room and, after Lily's discourteous behavior toward her handyman, Edna was surprised at the woman's affability. Their conversation was light and pleasant, and the time passed quickly before Clem appeared alongside the house, raising a hand to let them know he'd finished. The women left the comfort of the conservatory, Lily to call upstairs to the girls and Edna to speak to Clem.

"You did pick up a nail. I found the leak and plugged it, so you should be fine," he said.

"I don't need a new tire?" Edna was surprised and delighted at the news. "Let me pay you something for your work," she said, opening the car door to retrieve her tote.

"Most certainly not," Lily said, coming up behind Edna and folding her arms across her chest. She glared at Clem as if he'd been the one to suggest it.

Before Edna could speak, Amanda and Lettie came running up, so after again thanking both Clem and Lily for the rescue and the hospitality, she drove away from the house feeling slightly awkward. Maybe it was because Lily was so abrupt with him, but Edna was determined to find a way to repay Clem.

Chapter 5

"Lettie seems nice," Edna said to Amanda as she headed across town. The comment was partly to make conversation with her granddaughter, but she also was curious to learn what Amanda knew of the Beck family.

The girl nodded. "Yes."

It might be like a dental extraction to get any information, Edna thought with some amusement over the reticence of children. Aloud, she said, "How did you two become friends?"

Amanda turned to face her, brow crinkled. "What do you mean?"

"When people become friends, there's usually something that attracts them to each other, or something that happens to throw them together. Like ..." Edna thought for a minute. "Were you assigned to do a school project together?"

"Oh," Amanda said as understanding brightened her face. "No project. She lives near me."

"So you walk home together?" Edna knew that Irene drove her youngest child to school in the morning, mainly because Amanda tended to dawdle over her morning routine. Irene wanted to insure Amanda didn't dillydally once she was out of the house.

At Edna's question, Amanda merely nodded again, but then seemed to have forgotten the conversation as she stared out at the passing scenery. After a moment's silence, she turned to Edna with serious brown eyes. "It really isn't far, Gramma."

Taking only a second or two to realize what Amanda was talking about, Edna bit back a laugh at her granddaughter's reassurance that she wasn't walking miles every day. The elementary school was four blocks from Matthew and Irene's house. "It's nice of you to make friends with Lettie. I bet it wasn't easy for her to change schools in the middle of the year."

Amanda shrugged as if to say "no big deal" and returned her attention to the view. After a minute or two of companionable silence, she glanced back at Edna. "Can Lettie come over to play tomorrow?"

"If it's okay with her grandmother, she can."

The girl's eyes sparkled. "We can go to Mary's and play with the kittens."

Edna laughed. "If she isn't too busy."

"Oh, Mary's never too busy. She likes us to come over."

Edna chuckled again. It was true. Mary did enjoy having children visit. She loved to watch them play with the cats and Hank. Her animals seemed to like the attention, too. Benjamin received his share of petting from the grandchildren, but the newness of Mary's three additional cats drew the youngsters next door.

As Edna neared town and approached the grocery store, she had an idea she knew would please her granddaughter. "How about flatbread pizza for supper tonight?"

"Yeah," Amanda cheered, quickly adding, "Can I pick the toppings?"

For the next half hour, Edna strolled up and down the aisles, deciding what she might buy to augment her pantry supplies for a nine-year-old guest. While the girl took off for the produce area, Edna found tiny marshmallows for cocoa, cereal with more sugar than either she or Albert liked, and an assortment of snacks. She had reached the pet section when Amanda rounded the corner, holding out a large tomato. After waiting for Edna's approval, she scurried away in search of cheese. Edna was trying to decide which dry food to get for Benjamin when her granddaughter returned with a packet of mozzarella and another of sliced pepperoni.

"What would you like on yours, Gramma?" she said, her forehead furrowed with the seriousness of the question.

"Would you find a fresh green pepper for me, please? I need to get milk and eggs, then I think we're done."

On a Friday afternoon, even though they were ahead of most of the payday crowd, it took nearly twenty minutes to get through the checkout line and on the road again. When they reached the house, Edna had barely turned off the engine when Amanda jumped from the car.

"Can I go say hi to Mary?" she called.

"If you help take in the groceries, I think Mary will be in the kitchen before we have a chance to put everything away," Edna said.

Sure enough, Amanda had just put the carton of eggs into the refrigerator when Hank came wiggling into the room, head lowered and tail wagging his entire back end. Spot bounded in on his heels and jumped onto the chair next to Benjamin. As Amanda knelt to hug Hank's neck, Mary popped her head in the door. "Whatcha doin'?" she asked in her usual greeting.

"Hi, Mary." Edna grinned and winked at Amanda who looked up at her grandmother with wide brown eyes as if to say, "You were right."

Leaping to her feet, the youngster hurried to Mary who bent to receive the girl's embrace. Edna could see the flush of pleasure on the redhead's face.

"Come in, Mary. We're having flatbread pizza for supper. I hope you can join us."

When Mary didn't answer immediately, Amanda encouraged her. "Oh, yes, Mary. You gotta stay. You can choose your own toppings," she added, making it sound like a bribe.

Mary grinned. "Hard to refuse an invitation like that."

"First, let's have cocktails by a fire in the living room," Edna suggested, taking a bottle of cranberry juice from the fridge for Amanda's libation and reaching for a bottle of red wine for Mary and herself.

Amanda volunteered to put out one of the newly purchased snack mixes, while Mary offered to light the prepared fire in the living room hearth. They were nicely settled when Edna heard the front door open.

"Anyone home," called a familiar voice.

"Auntie Starling," cried Amanda, jumping to her feet to follow Hank into the hall.

"What are you doing here, kiddo?" Starling's voice preceded her into the room as she appeared with an arm around her niece's shoulders and a hand scratching the black Lab's head.

"I'm staying with Gramma 'til Monday," Amanda announced proudly.

Edna and Mary rose to greet the youngest of the Davies children before Edna went to fetch another glass from the kitchen.

"To what do I owe this pleasure?" she asked her daughter, returning to hand her the wine. "It's wonderful to see you, but I didn't expect you this weekend."

"Charlie's taking me to dinner tomorrow night for an early Valentine's treat since he's on duty all next week. When I heard about the storm moving in, I thought I'd drive down early and spend the weekend."

Starling was a mix of her parents, long-legged and slim like Albert with Edna's auburn hair and brown eyes. She lived in Boston's Back Bay and was half-owner of an art gallery where she displayed framed photos of New England people and places, mostly historic, and where her partner sold his oil paintings of sights around Boston and Cambridge.

She plopped down on the sofa next to Mary as Amanda resumed her place on the rug with her back against the arm of the couch and Hank stretched out beside her. Starling waited for Benjamin to jump into her lap before taking a sip of her wine. Stroking the ginger cat, she looked fondly down at the top of her niece's head and spoke to Edna. "With Dad gone, I thought you'd be alone. Nice to see Manda-Panda here."

At Starling's pet name for her, the girl tilted back her head and grinned up at her aunt.

"Tell me about the storm. I haven't tuned in the news today," Edna said. "What's the latest forecast?"

"'Bout four inches, they're sayin'," Mary answered

before Starling could reply. "Rain first, turning to sleet, then snow, so the roads will be nice and slippery."

"Brrr," Starling grumbled. "I'm ready for spring." She gently ruffled Amanda's hair. "What's the news from Poppy and Matt?" she asked, using the name that Dean, the youngest grandchild, had dubbed Albert during the family's Christmas visit. "How's the fishing trip going?"

"Let's call 'em," Amanda said, tilting her head again to study her aunt's face.

"After supper," Edna said. Correctly reading the restlessness in her neighbor, she went on, "Right now, I think Mary has something to tell you."

The redhead's face lit up with her chance to tell about the ghost, while Amanda's eyes grew wide and Starling refrained from laughing at the idea. Edna guessed her daughter didn't want to spoil Mary's story by announcing that there was no such thing as ghosts. Also, the rebel theory probably delighted Starling who was an avid student of New England history.

Who am I to naysay, Edna thought as Mary was describing the unusual sounds she heard.

"Can you come over tonight and help me investigate?" Mary concluded.

Before her daughter or granddaughter got carried away with the idea, Edna spoke up. "Maybe another time, Mary. I don't want Amanda to be up all night if she's expecting her friend to visit tomorrow." Before too many groans of protest could emanate from the others, Edna stood. "Ready to make pizzas?"

The evening passed quickly. After supper, Mary took Hank and Spot home to see what mischief her house cats had "gotten themselves into," as she put it. Edna took Amanda and Starling into her office where they used the speaker phone to reach Albert, Matthew, Roger and Ken in Florida. After much joking and laughing and tall tales, the call ended, and Edna thought a mug of hot cider with a cinnamon stick stirrer would help quiet Amanda and allow her to sleep.

When the youngster had finally been tucked into bed, Edna and Starling sat for a while longer before the dying embers of the fire.

Starling was stretched out on the sofa with Benjamin curled in her lap. "Amanda's having a friend over tomorrow?" she asked, breaking the easy silence.

Edna nodded as she continued to gaze at the fire, her mind occupied with the earlier events of the day.

"I didn't know she had friends in this area." Starling seemed intent on grabbing Edna's attention.

Edna mentally shook herself back into the room and turned to her daughter. "She hasn't. This is a new friend who happens to be visiting her own grandmother this week."

"So who is she, this new friend of Manda-Panda's?"

Realizing it would be good to voice her recent thoughts, Edna gave Starling the long version of Amanda's unplanned visit, beginning with Irene's call the previous morning. In explaining Irene's concerns about Rosie Beck, Edna reminded Starling about the scandal that had been front-page news.

"So, are you talking about Rosie *Haverstrum*?" Starling suddenly showed more interest. "Wow. That was quite a story. Knocked this town on its ear, at the time." She pushed herself up straighter, causing

Benjamin to jump down and head for his bed next to the warm hearth. "You know her mother?"

Edna nodded. "Lily Beck. She's a long-time member of the garden club. By the way, Rosie took her maiden name back. She goes by Rosie Beck now." Edna looked thoughtful for a few seconds. "I don't know what surname Lettie goes by. I wonder if Irene would know. I don't want to assume and cause the child any embarrassment if she hasn't kept her father's name."

"Speaking of the dead, have you ever mentioned your sleuthing escapades to Dad?" Starling's eyes twinkled. Edna guessed that, as they say of a good lawyer, Starling wasn't asking a question to which she didn't already know the answer.

Edna scowled, taking what she knew to be bait but rising to it anyway. "You're perfectly aware that I haven't, nor do I intend to. What's past is past, and there's no need to stir up old troubles unnecessarily. Besides, it would be much too complicated to explain everything to him at this late date. He'd only worry."

Chapter 6

Saturday morning dawned cold and windy, but sunny. There was no sign of the predicted storm until Edna stepped outside to fetch the newspaper from the front stoop. Decidedly, there was a smell of snow in the frigid air. Starling and Amanda clattered downstairs as Edna poured her first cup of coffee. The consensus was for a waffle breakfast with bacon, after which Edna settled at the kitchen table with a final cup of coffee and the daily crossword while Amanda and Starling went next door to visit Mary and her menagerie.

But Edna couldn't keep her mind on the puzzle this morning. She'd slept restlessly. At one point, she dreamed she was wandering from room to room in a maze. She was trying to find her way out into the open air, but each door she passed through only led to an increasingly dark and stuffy interior. Suddenly, she found herself in the center of a crowd. Wherever she looked, people were glaring at her, pointing and shouting words she couldn't make out. One woman picked something up from the ground and threw it at her. Others followed suit until everyone seemed to be hurling objects at her. She found herself backing against a wall. Stones banged against the surface, barely missing her. Her feet stuck to the floor, so she could only bob and weave, dodging the flying debris. She finally awoke with a start, struggling against the sheets she'd gotten wrapped around herself. The hammering was caused by something, probably a tree branch, hitting the side of the house as a fierce wind picked up outside. That had been at four in the morning, and, heart racing, she'd been unable to get back to sleep. Now, in the bright morning light, she restlessly set aside the newspaper and took her coffee into the office.

At her desk, she turned on the computer, but instead of opening her e-mail messages, the way she usually began her morning, she resumed her search for articles having to do with "Haverstrum." Probably because she'd refreshed her memory of Rosie's tale by retelling it to Starling the night before, Edna hadn't been able to get the drama out of her dreams or off her mind. Too many questions tumbled over each other in her head.

Why had the police narrowed in on Rosie? Because she was the murdered man's wife and, therefore, the most obvious? Edna knew from her television programs, the victim's spouse usually had the most to gain and was, therefore, the prime suspect. In the Haverstrum case, the police apparently hadn't found strong enough proof of Rosie's guilt or they would have arrested her instead of only bringing her in for questioning.

Edna thought back to her own situation and wondered if the townsfolk would still be shunning her, had Tom Greene's killer not been found. What would her life be like with an unsolved murder hanging over her? She could only imagine what Rosie Beck and her daughter were suffering. Before Edna questioned Charlie or Mary about what they knew of the case, she wanted to read everything she could about the personalities involved.

What about other suspects? Had there been sufficient evidence to suspect someone else? Farren McCree, for instance. Edna entered Rosie's former best friend's name into the Google search box and began a new hunt.

The thirty-nine-year-old McCree worked at the nursery that had hired Rosie. They had been working side-by-side for over a year and had developed a social friendship when Farren began her affair with Gregory. Less trusting than Gregory's wife, when the affair began to cool, Farren had followed Haverstrum and caught him wining and dining the young woman he had recently employed as his office assistant. To get even, Farren mentioned her suspicions to Rosie about young Bobbi Callahan, a sophomore at the nearby university.

Before Edna got side-tracked with the young girlfriend, she clicked on one of the items that had come up for Farren McCree. In part, the article was a rundown of her actions on the days leading up to the discovery of Haverstrum's body. It revealed no more than what Rosie had told Edna. Farren had reportedly visited Gregory Haverstrum's apartment on the afternoon he died, but hadn't stayed long.

Edna was disappointed. Nothing much of significance was divulged, so she closed the article, making a mental note to ask both Mary and Charlie what they knew of the woman. Edna was scanning other McCree items for any detail she might have missed, when she heard voices coming from the kitchen. She switched the screen to her message in-box just before Amanda came rushing into the room, followed seconds later by Starling.

Edna didn't feel guilty about investigating the scandal or the people involved, but she didn't know if Amanda knew about the case or about Lettie's family's history. If the subject ever arose, Edna would rather talk face-to-face with her granddaughter than have the child see lists of news headlines with her friend's name on a computer screen.

"Can we call Lettie now?" Amanda said, picking up Benjamin from the chair beside the desk. She draped the ginger cat over her shoulder and stroked his back as she sat down. He, apparently, didn't like this new arrangement because he eased himself onto the chair back and pushed off from Amanda's shoulder onto the window ledge where he sat in a small spot of sun and began to wash a front paw.

Edna was surprised to see by her desk clock that it was nearly ten. "I think it's late enough. Let me find my garden club list of phone numbers." As she hunted through papers in a basket beside the computer monitor, she asked, "What are you planning to do today?"

Amanda shrugged. "I dunno. Play with the kittens, I guess."

Starling, leaning against the door jamb, hands thrust into the pockets of her blue woolen slacks, said, "How about a drive to Point Judith Lighthouse? The waves will be amazing in this wind. We could go to Iggy's for lunch. What do you say? They have the best clamcakes," she added as if to persuade her niece.

Amanda's eyes lit up. "Yeah. Cool, Auntie Starling."

Without looking up from what she was doing, Edna

said, "Pick another lunch place. The Iggy's at Point Judith closes for the winter." Ignoring the resulting duet of groans, Edna found the phone list and glanced over at Amanda. "If we ask Lettie, we should invite her grandmother, too."

"I guess," Amanda said with a definite lack of enthusiasm.

Starling chuckled at her niece's lackluster reply and said, "Sure. Why not?"

Lily answered on the third ring. After preliminary greetings, Edna mentioned their plans for the morning, asking if she and Lettie would like to join them.

"I have some things to do today, but I'm sure Violet would enjoy the outing. All she's done since breakfast is sit around and play with her phone."

Edna had the impression that Lettie was within earshot of her grandmother's remark. "I'm sorry you're not able to join us, but we'll be by in half an hour to get Violet." Edna was careful to use the name Lily seemed to insist on calling her granddaughter. Hanging up, she studied Amanda's scoop-necked jersey and light cardigan, "The wind will be stronger and colder near the water. You might want to wear your hoodie."

"Okay." Amanda jumped up, heading into the hall and up the stairs.

Starling slipped into the chair vacated by her niece. Benjamin stepped gingerly from the window sill to her shoulder and slid into her lap. She scratched along his jawline, but seemed preoccupied.

"What's on your mind, dear?" Edna prompted.

Starling's focus came back to the room and her brow creased. "Mary's pretty serious about that ghost of hers."

"Yes, I know."

"I don't think she's had much sleep lately. She asked me if we could all stay with her tonight. Made it sound like a game, but I think she'd really like someone in the house with her. Knowing her, she's dying to investigate. I'm surprised she doesn't want to do it alone. I thought she was braver than that." Starling looked at Edna questioningly as she absently stroked Benjamin's back.

"She might be intimidated by the unknown in her old familiar surroundings," Edna said, returning the phone list to the basket. "I thought you might enjoy her theory of the Colonial rebel in her old nursery. Did you tell her you'd join her tonight?"

Starling laughed. "I was fascinated with her tale." She then grew serious and shook her head. "I would help her out, but I'm having dinner with Charlie tonight."

"Did she hear the stomping again last night?"

Starling nodded. "Maybe I can go over tomorrow night." A sudden twinkle came into her eyes. "I wonder if Charlie would like to help."

Edna laughed. "He just might." She sobered then. "Tomorrow is Amanda's last night here. I'll be driving her home Monday morning." She paused and studied Starling thoughtfully. "Unless you're heading back to Boston on Monday and could drop her off on your way?" She turned the thought into a question and then added, "I'll spend the night with Mary, but not while Amanda's here. I may be selfish, not wanting to share her, but it's not often that I have her to myself, and it's an added bonus that you're also here this weekend. As much as I sympathize with Mary, her ghost can wait."

Starling smiled. "I understand." She paused for a minute as if reflecting before she continued. "Sure. I can drive Manda-Panda home, but I'll have to leave early. I'm opening the studio on Monday. Gary is meeting with a new client in Marblehead, so I'm watching the shop," she said, mentioning her partner who occasionally worked on commission to paint a landscape for someone who wanted to memorialize a house, garden or favorite ocean view.

"I'll phone Mary when we get back after lunch. I'm sure she'll be fine during the day, and I'll make arrangements to stay with her some night next week." Edna rose from her chair as she heard Amanda bouncing down the stairs. "I feel certain what Mary's hearing is the old house settling. She may think she knows all the sounds, but as wood dries and weather takes its toll, things shift and new noises crop up." She smiled at her daughter and changed the subject. "Right now, will you drive or shall I?"

When they got to Lily's house, Lettie was already waiting on the veranda. As she ran down the steps, Lily appeared in the doorway, a shawl around her shoulders. She waved to them. In the passenger's seat, Edna waved back. After opening the car door for her friend, Amanda scooted over and, once the girls were safely buckled up, Starling put the car in gear and they were on their way.

The wind was stronger than Edna expected when they arrived at Point Judith. Roiling waves crashed onto the gravel, sending salt spray over the rocks that edged the parking lot. "Maybe this was a mistake. Shall we go someplace where there's more shelter?"

She could have saved her breath because the girls were already tumbling out of the back seat and moving toward the wider stretch of beach beyond the lighthouse. Several more cars were in the lot, but their inhabitants were content to stay inside and watch the waves. Nobody seemed to be as adventurous as Amanda and Lettie.

"I'll go with them," Starling said, opening her door. "I'm guessing they won't stay out in this wind for long."

Edna looked out to sea, enjoying the storm-tossed water and waves from the comfort of the car. As time when by and the others didn't return, she grew restless. Turning in her seat, she could see nobody and decided they must have walked farther down the rocky shore. Resigned to wait and not worry, at least for the moment, she pulled a sketch pad and pen from her tote bag and began to draw. Her memory and artist's eye enabled her to make a fairly good representation of the Christmas Rose that had recently bloomed in Lily's garden and of which the woman was inordinately proud.

So focused was she on what she was doing, Edna was startled when the car doors opened and the girls toppled in.

"Brrr," Starling said, starting the engine and turning up the heat. "That wind is cold."

On her way across the seat to make room for Lettie, Amanda glanced over Edna's shoulder. "What are you drawing, Gramma?"

Her question made Lettie lean over the seat to see, too. "It looks like Lily's plant," the youngster remarked.

"It's a strawberry blossom," Amanda said.

"It does resemble a strawberry blossom, doesn't it?"

Edna agreed, holding up the sketch so the girls could see it before she closed the cover on the pad. "You can't tell from my drawing, but it's larger than a strawberry plant and the leaves are different. Lettie guessed it. I've drawn the Christmas Rose that grows in her grandmother's garden. It's a present for Lily."

"Why is it called Christmas Rose?" Amanda asked, folding her arms across Starling's seat back and resting her cold-reddened cheek on her forearm.

"According to Mrs. Rabichek's journal, the legend claims that it sprouted in the snow from the tears of a young girl who had no gift to give the Christ child in Bethlehem," Edna said.

While she tucked the pad back into her tote, Lettie and Amanda sat back and fastened their seat belts. As they were buckling up, Lettie said, "Lily dries those in the oven."

"Why?" Amanda asked.

"She crumbles 'em up and keeps 'em in jars. Kinda like spices."

"What do they taste like?"

"Dunno."

"Why not?"

"She says it's medicine." Lettie sounded as if she were tired of the subject.

"Like for headaches or something?" Amanda said.

"Not sure," Lettie said, ending the conversation with a bored tone.

Edna frowned but didn't turn around. She wouldn't make a big deal of it with the girls, but she knew the plant was highly poisonous. She made a mental note to ask Lily about her "medicine," the next chance she got.

She wondered if the woman realized how dangerous it was to trust anything made from her garden plants. The strength of a single dose can vary so much with the growing season.

Chapter 7

After leaving the lighthouse parking lot, Starling chose to drive along Sand Hill Cove Road to Galilee where they stopped at the Champlin's seafood market. Edna bought cooked lobster meat, smoked bluefish and fresh clams while the girls and Starling strolled along the wharf to look at the boats. The Block Island ferry wouldn't be leaving until later that afternoon, but there was plenty of activity along the docks as fishermen tended to their boats and tourists took photos of each other with the choppy sea as background.

When she finished shopping, Edna joined the girls. "Do you want to stay for a while and walk along the beach?"

Before her niece could answer, Starling said, "I'm for heading home and some hot clam chowder. I've had enough of this cold wind."

"Me, too," Amanda agreed. She turned to Lettie who was looking at her cell phone display and didn't seem to have heard. Amanda rolled her eyes at Starling and Edna, heaved a sigh and took her friend by the arm to lead her toward the car. The youngster complied complacently without looking up from the device in her hand, although Edna noticed a smile twitch at the sides of Lettie's mouth.

At home, Edna busied herself in the kitchen while

Starling lit a fire in the living room grate. The girls, after changing into lighter weight jerseys and sweaters, set up a card table near the hearth. Deciding on Parcheesi, they sat down to play until lunch was ready.

"Is that phone ever out of her hand?" Starling asked, reaching around Edna to snatch a lump of lobster meat from the salad bowl.

Edna knew it was a rhetorical question, so didn't answer as she toasted hot dog buns for the seafood rolls and stirred milk into the warming chowder. Instead, she said, "By the time you set the table and ask the girls to wash their hands, lunch should be ready." She didn't mention her house rule of "no phones at the table" to her daughter, assuming Amanda would let her friend know without having to be reminded by Starling.

When they entered the kitchen, however, Lettie laid her mobile next to her plate before sitting down.

"Please put that away," Edna said, setting the platter of lobster rolls in the middle of the table.

"Told you," Amanda admonished her friend.

Lettie looked up at Edna with eyes wide in a near panic. "But Mommy might text me," she almost wailed.

"Come with me," Edna said with a gentle smile that she hoped would mask the impatience she felt. Apparently, the child's mother kept her on an electronic leash. Preceding the girl into her office, Edna picked up a pencil and wrote her phone number on a slip of paper. "You can either phone your mother or text her, but please give her my number. Tell her we are sitting down to eat. If she needs to contact you in the next half hour or so, she can phone this house."

Lettie looked baffled, but did as she was told,

sending her mother a text message. Obeying Edna's instruction, she left the phone on the desk and followed Edna back to the kitchen. Over hot chowder and toasted lobster rolls, she soon seemed to forget her distress. The morning's venture had certainly stimulated appetites, including Edna's. Everyone ate hungrily with only occasional murmurings of appreciation breaking the silence.

After lunch, as soon as the girls were excused from the table, Lettie ran to the office to check her phone. Starling went upstairs to her room, and Edna decided to sit by the fire to read. At Edna's request, Amanda and Lettie cleaned up the lunch dishes before returning to the living room to resume their game. They had played for only a few minutes when Amanda spoke to her friend, apparently voicing something that had been on her mind.

"Why do you call your grandmother 'Lily'?"

"She wants me to. Mommy calls her Lily, too."

"Why does she call you Violet instead of Lettie?"

"She says we were named after pretty flowers, and that's what we should be called, not some silly nicknames."

Smiling to herself and holding back a chuckle, Edna returned her attention to her book. When she realized she'd been staring at the same paragraph for the last five minutes, she decided to check her e-mail messages and went to her office. Twenty minutes later, Amanda came in and threw herself down in the chair beside the desk. Fortunately, Benjamin was asleep in his bed beside the hearth and so wasn't ousted by the youngster.

Edna looked over from the monitor at the scowling face of her granddaughter. "What's wrong, kiddo?"

Slouched in the chair, Amanda stared at her legs stretched out before her. "Lettie."

"What about Lettie?"

"She's not playing. She keeps sending messages to her mom."

"Does she do that all the time? I thought her mother was working. How does she find the time to text back?"

Amanda shrugged and turned eyes filled with frustration on Edna. "When it's my turn, she grabs her phone and then when it's her turn, I have to wait for her to finish texting." Huffily, she crossed her arms over her chest and returned to studying her pants legs. When Edna didn't say anything, Amanda looked up at her. "Let's take her back to her grandmother's."

Edna sympathized with her granddaughter's annoyance, but nearly burst out laughing at the child's solution to her problem. "Have you asked Lettie to put her phone away while you're playing?"

Chin now lowered to her chest, Amanda moved her head in what Edna took for a nod. "It doesn't do any good. She says her mom worries if she doesn't hear from her."

"Do you think it might be Lettie who needs to stay connected to her mother?"

Amanda's eyes were on her feet as she tapped the sides of her shoes together. A few seconds went by before she said, "I suppose."

"Did you know Lettie's father died a couple of years ago?"

Still watching her sneakers, Amanda nodded.

"Sometimes when children lose a parent, they get frightened about losing the other parent. Do you think that's what might be going on, that Lettie's afraid her mother might go away?"

Amanda glanced at Edna with curiosity. "Maybe."

At that moment, they heard a noise in the hall and the object of their discussion appeared in the doorway. "It's your turn," Lettie said with a note of impatience.

Amanda sat up straighter, pulling her legs in. "I'm going to see if Mary's home." As she stood, she added, "I want to play with the kittens."

"Me, too," Lettie said, her face lighting up with anticipation.

"You have to leave your phone here, though," Amanda said sternly.

"Mommy doesn't like it if I don't answer right away. She worries."

Edna wondered if Amanda might be wrong about who mainly initiated the texts between mother and daughter. Could it be that Rosie was afraid something might happen to Lettie and had to check on her constantly? "Why don't you text your mother and tell her to call me if she needs to talk to you? She has my number."

Before Lettie had time to respond to the suggestion, Edna heard Starling hurrying down the stairs. At the same time, the doorbell rang.

"I'll get it," Starling called out seconds before Edna heard the front door open.

At the sound of muffled voices, Lettie disappeared into the hall with Amanda not far behind.

Curious as to who had just arrived, Edna got up and followed the girls into the hall in time to see Rosie hug her daughter. She was laughing, as if delighted to have played a trick on Lettie. "Surprised to see me, sweetie?"

"Hello, Rosie," Edna said, approaching the group at the front door. "I thought you were working this weekend." *She must have been texting while driving*, Edna thought with disapproval.

The woman shook her head, still obviously pleased with herself. "It's Saturday. I decided to take the night off. I missed my little girl and thought I'd drive down ahead of the snow to spend some time with her." She tilted her head toward the outside. "Looks like I just made it." To Lettie, she said, "Why don't you go get your things? I want to reach Lily's before the roads start to ice up."

Edna wondered about the reason Lettie was visiting Lily in the first place. Hadn't Rosie claimed she'd be too busy to take any time off for the next week? Shaking the idea from her mind--after all, Rosie's schedule was none of Edna's business--she introduced Starling to Lettie's mother before asking, "Would you like a cup of tea before you go?"

"I'd better not take the time. Lettie won't be long."

The three women chatted about the weather and road conditions for the few minutes it took the girls to fetch Lettie's backpack. By the time the youngster retrieved her jacket, hat and gloves from the coat closet, Rosie was reaching for the doorknob.

"Whew, that was fast," Starling said when the door had closed behind mother and daughter. She put an arm around Amanda's shoulders, turning her toward the living room. "I hereby challenge you to a game of Parcheesi, Manda-Panda."

The girl had apparently forgotten all about visiting

Mary and the kittens as she smiled up at her aunt and walked with her down the hall.

"When is Charlie picking you up for dinner?" Edna called to Starling.

"He's not." Starling glanced back over her shoulder with a pout. "He called just before Lettie's mother arrived and said he has to work tonight. They're expecting emergency conditions and want all available personnel on duty. We're postponing our dinner date," she said, adding with emphasis and a roll of her eyes, "*again*." She turned abruptly to face Edna and scowled. "Did you have this much trouble trying to get a date with Dad when he was on call at the hospital?"

Edna was taken aback for a second or two and nearly whooped with delight. *Is this a hint that something more serious is going on between her and Charlie?* Edna wondered, but didn't want to push the matter at that moment. Starling would confide in her when the time was right, or clam up, if it weren't. Instead, Edna said, "I'll call Mary and see if she'd like to come for supper."

"What are we having?" Amanda asked, pausing in the archway, and the look passing between mother and daughter broke.

"How about chicken pot pie?" Edna suggested, her glance lowering to her granddaughter's face. "Comfort food for a cold night."

The resounding cheers from her daughter and granddaughter made her laugh, but as they disappeared into the living room, she wondered if she'd have a chance to get Mary alone long enough to ask what she knew about the Haverstrum and Beck scandal.

Chapter 8

After a deep and dreamless sleep, Edna awoke and rose early. The storm had ended, leaving six inches of snow in its wake. Glancing out the window at the scene below, she saw that the Benton brothers, neighborhood teenagers who shoveled for the Davies and Mary without having to be phoned each time, had already cleared the drive. Edna idly wondered if they were on break this week or had they dragged themselves out of bed on one of the few mornings they could sleep in. She made a mental note to add a generous tip when they came around to collect.

Going down to the kitchen, she made coffee and took a cup to her office. She wanted to resume her search of news about Gregory Haverstrum before Amanda and Starling came down for breakfast, but the computer hadn't finished booting up when the doorbell rang. Surprised, she looked at the wall clock and realized it wasn't yet eight o'clock.

"Who in the world ..." she muttered, hurrying into the front hall.

Before she reached the door, she heard muffled banging, as if gloved hands were pounding on the wood. A faint voice called through the heavy wood, "Edna? Edna, are you up. Please let me in." The doorbell rang again.

Tuck? Recognizing the voice, Edna grew increasingly agitated by the urgency in her friend's tone. She fumbled with the deadbolt.

"Tuck?" Edna finally had the door open. Frowning, she wondered what had brought her friend to the house, and why she seemed so distressed. "Was I supposed to join you in church this morning?" She tried to remember if she'd forgotten a previous engagement with all that had been distracting her for the past few days.

Ignoring the question, Tuck pushed past her into the hall, unwrapping a cashmere scarf from her neck as she did so. "Oh, Edna, something terrible has happened." Tuck always wore a slightly puzzled expression as if not certain how she had gotten where she was. This morning, her eyes, the same sky blue as her scarf, appeared both frightened and bewildered. She stripped off her jacket, and Edna saw how upset Tuck must've been when she dressed. Usually so meticulously turned out, Tuck seemed to have pulled on an old pair of navy blue stretch pants and a light green turtleneck. Edna's attention was drawn away from Tuck's clothing at her friend's next words. "Peppa's been arrested," she blurted, plopping down on a nearby ladder-back chair.

"Arrested? For what?" Edna couldn't imagine Peppa doing anything unlawful.

"Vehicular homicide."

That one, Edna could believe. Having been a passenger in Peppa's vintage Mercedes when they'd first met, Edna managed to repeat the harrowing experience only twice in the last year and a half. True, the woman was quite reckless behind the wheel, but miraculously had avoided having an accident in over fifty years.

Tickets for speeding, running red lights and ignoring stop signs were a different matter, but she always paid promptly and cheerfully.

"My goodness." Shocked by the news, Edna needed time to absorb what she'd just heard. "I knew it was bound to happen sooner or later, but *homicide*." Her voice rose on this last word, making it sound like a question.

Tuck nodded as she removed her overcoat and pulled off her snow-caked boots.

"Come into the kitchen. The coffee's fresh," Edna said, feeling numb and wanting to sit before her knees gave way.

In the kitchen, instead of sitting, Tuck paced and babbled, apparently talking more to herself than to Edna. "She's got old Dick Feinberg to represent her. He's not a criminal attorney, but they've known each other for years. She phoned me this morning after she called him. Officially, she's only allowed one phone call, but most of them at the station are her Saturday morning kids, you know."

They and half the town, Edna thought and almost felt like smiling. If there was anyone in the area who hadn't attended Peppa's weekend story hour, they hadn't grown up locally.

"You've got to go talk to her."

"To Peppa?" Edna was confused. When Tuck merely gave a curt nod, Edna asked, "Why me?" She realized her question sounded like she was reluctant to speak with her friend, but before she could amend it, Tuck spoke.

"Because she's not speaking to me at the moment."

Edna shook her head, trying to decipher Tuck's convoluted way of thinking. "I thought you said she phoned you this morning."

"She did, but when she found out I knew Clem was back in town, she got angry and hung up on me. I called back, but was told she wouldn't come to the phone. I even went over to the station. That's where I was before I came here. She's flat out refusing to see me."

"Clem?" Edna couldn't imagine there was more than one man in town with the name, but it was too coincidental. "You mean the 'Clem' who works for Lily Beck?"

Tuck nodded. "Peppa's ex." Her tone implied Edna was already supposed to know, but in the relatively short time she'd known Peppa, the woman hadn't discussed her former husband or anything about the divorce. She definitely hadn't spoken his name.

"What has he to do with it?"

"He's the man she ran over last night, the reason she's been arrested."

This last pronouncement was too much for Edna. "Hold on, Tuck. I need you to take a deep breath, then sit down and tell me what's going on. From the beginning, please," she added as she herself sat at the kitchen table.

Tuck did as she was told, taking a minute to stroke Benjamin's golden fur. In the seat next to hers, the cat blinked sleepily, having been awakened by the commotion. Seeming slightly more relaxed, Tuck stared down at the coffee Edna placed before her and began her tale.

"Peppa's call woke me. I didn't realize she was

calling from the police station. I wasn't wearing my glasses, you see, so hadn't looked at the caller ID before picking up."

Edna knew Tuck was apt to go off on a tangent and lose her train of thought, so she prompted. "What did Peppa tell you?"

"That she found a body at the foot of her driveway this morning." Tuck raised her eyebrows and lifted her shoulders as if totally baffled. "I thought she was joking, so I laughed and waited for her to deliver the punch line. She got huffy and said she wasn't kidding. That's when she mentioned she was calling from the police station. She'd already phoned Dick and was waiting for him to show up. She wanted me to know what had happened, in case they put her in jail. Asked if I could go over to her place and take care of Rufus."

An image of Peppa's large but gentle and loving Rottweiler popped into Edna head. "Will you take him to your house?"

Tuck took a sip of coffee and thought for several seconds, frowning as if the idea hadn't occurred to her. Then, she nodded. "I will if Peppa's not released today. He'll be all right in the backyard, but I'd hate to think of him all alone, waiting for her to come home. Don't you think that would be sad?"

Time to get Tuck back on track, Edna thought, more confused than ever. "You said she ran over her ex-husband last night and found a body in her driveway this morning. His body?"

"Of course," Tuck said, as if it were plain as day. "That's the problem. Because of how bitter she's always been, everyone's going to think she ran him down on purpose."

Edna thought Tuck was probably right, but didn't say anything as her friend continued.

"Peppa said she remembered the car bouncing over a snow mound when she turned into her driveway last night. She'd been out to dinner with friends and got home late. You know she always has a glass or two of wine with dinner," Tuck added.

Before she could go off on Peppa's drinking habits, Edna said, "There's usually a pile of snow in the gutter after the plows have been by. I bet she gunned the engine and swerved into the driveway. She does that even in good weather." Having followed Peppa home on several occasions, Edna pictured Peppa's erratic driving habits.

"That's what she said. Not about her racing the car, but about thinking the snow had been left by the street plows. I was supposed to pick her up for church this morning, so she thought she'd get out early and clear it away before I got there." Tuck paused and set her cup back on the table. "She's so thoughtful."

Edna ignored Tuck's last remark, so horrific was the image that popped into her head. "And instead of a pile of snow, she found the body of her ex-husband?"

Tears filled Tuck's eyes and she fumbled for a pocket before realizing there were none in her stretch pants. Edna, having already noticed what Tuck was doing, pushed up from the table and retrieved a box of tissue from beside the sink. Resuming her seat, she laid the box where Tuck could reach it.

Tuck nodded in appreciation and, having had a minute to compose herself, pulled out a tissue and dabbed away tears before speaking again. "Peppa said she didn't realize who it was. Just that she saw the body of a man, so she ran back into the house to call nine-one-one. After talking to the dispatcher, she went back out to see if he might be alive, but the police had told her not to touch him. He was lying face down, so she didn't see his face until after the police arrived. The fire and rescue truck pulled up right behind them. They were the ones who turned him over. She was already in shock over what she had done, but then the police asked her if she could identify the guy. She had no idea until they asked her to look at the body that it was Clem." As if exhausted by the telling, Tuck sat back in her chair and reached over to stroke Benjamin's back.

Edna thought about what she'd just heard as she sipped her coffee, now almost cold. She grimaced at the mug and put it aside before looking over at her friend. "You said you knew Clem was in town, but Peppa didn't?"

Slumped in her chair, Tuck looked utterly miserable. "When she told me it was Clem, she sounded really and truly stunned. Five years ago, when Peppa kicked him out, he moved to Springfield to live with his father and brother. She'd told him that she wouldn't have anything to do with him until he stopped drinking and straightened himself up."

"Is that why they divorced? He had a drinking problem?" Edna thought back to the man she'd met at Lily's. Yes, she could see that he might have been a recovering alcoholic from his thin frame and deeply lined skin, but he'd also looked fit and healthy.

"That's right." Tuck looked up at Edna. "She told

me she hasn't heard from him in all that time, that she didn't want to know anything about him unless he was sober. I told her he hadn't touched a drop of alcohol since the night of that near-fatal accident five years ago last Christmas. She asked me how I knew, and I had to confess that I'd run into him at Lily Beck's last November. He's been living above her garage for the last six months."

Edna thought of how gentle and friendly Clem had seemed, but didn't interrupt Tuck to say she'd met him at Lily's, too.

"Peppa asked me why I hadn't told her, and I said because he asked me not to. He wasn't ready to face her. I don't know what he was waiting for, but I respected his wishes. Peppa thinks I should have been loyal to her, not to Clem, so she hung up on me. You know how stubborn she can be. Now she's not speaking to me and I don't know what to do. Will you go see her and make her understand my side?"

"Before I do that, I need to know why you didn't tell Peppa. I thought you two were the best of friends. Why so loyal to Clem?"

"Because he was as much a friend as Peppa, at least at one time." Tuck gave a deep sigh. "Clem was a botany professor at the university. Nip hired him when we built our herb garden off the kitchen patio," Tuck said, speaking of her deceased husband. "The two men hit it off so well, that's when we started seeing Clem and Peppa socially. So, you see, I really knew Clem before I met Peppa. She's one of my best and dearest of friends, but I also feel a great deal of loyalty to Clem, particularly since he was trying so hard to reform."

Edna was wondering what she ought to do when she heard the shower go on upstairs. "My girls are getting up. Will you join us for breakfast. I need some time to absorb what you've told me. Perhaps later we can discuss what I should do."

Tuck shook her head and rose to her feet. "Thanks, Edna, but I can't stay. I need to go see about Rufus." She paused, looking more baffled than usual. "Do you think the police will let me near the house?"

Edna followed her friend to the hall, promising to talk to Peppa, if she could, but after Tuck had gone, it was Lily who came to Edna's mind.

Has anyone told her that her handyman is dead?

Chapter 9

"Who were you talking to?" Starling said, entering the kitchen ten minutes later and looking around the room as if expecting to see someone else.

"Helen Tucker," Edna said abstractedly. "She left while you were in the shower."

Leaning back against the edge of the kitchen sink, coffee mug in hand, Edna had been mulling over Tuck's news. Before she could explain further, Starling surprised her.

"Was she here about Peppa's accident last night?"

"How did you know?"

"I had a text from Charlie on my phone this morning. He asked me to call him when I got up. He told me Peppa might have killed her ex-husband. Isn't that awful?" Starling paused as she poured herself a cup of coffee and then looked over at Edna. "Actually, it's you he wants to talk to and as soon as possible, so I invited him to join us for breakfast." She looked anxious, as if Edna might object, given the horrifying news of the morning. "You don't mind, do you?"

Knowing her daughter conspired to spend as much time as she could with the police detective, Edna nearly laughed at Starling's transparency. "Of course not," she answered, although she knew a reply hadn't been necessary. "What are you making us for breakfast?"

Starling choked on her coffee, as if she'd swallowed a too-hot mouthful, and Edna did laugh this time. She knew her daughter to be a willing and adequate cook, but since her children were grown and had homes of their own, Edna hardly ever asked one of them to cook in her kitchen. This morning, she'd been half joking with her youngest child, but said, "I'll make popovers if you do the rest."

"Yummm. My favorite breakfast treat," Starling said, raising her eyebrows in delight. "I'll make bacon and scrambled eggs to go with them."

"And I think I also have some oranges to make fresh juice."

Starling chuckled. "It sounds perfect. I'll start the bacon. I bet the smell will stir Manda-Panda's taste buds. She might even make it downstairs before Charlie gets here."

As Starling began to turn toward the cupboard where the frying pans were stored, Edna put a restraining hand on her forearm. Leaning toward her daughter, she said in a low voice, "No talk of death, accidents or murder in front of Amanda, please. If Charlie wants to talk to me about Peppa's situation, I'd appreciate it if you'd take your niece to Mary's after breakfast."

Starling nodded, all humor gone. "Good idea." Five minutes later, when the doorbell rang, she hurried to greet Charlie. Edna moved to the stove to tend to Starling's abandoned frying pan, certain that her daughter would pass the suggestion along to Charlie, as soon as "good morning's" were out of the way.

The three adults barely had time to fill their coffee

mugs before Amanda was heard talking to Benjamin in the hallway. When the youngster entered the kitchen with the cat slung over her shoulder, any chance of serious talk was forgotten for the next half hour.

After breakfast, when Starling suggested they visit the neighbor's menagerie, Amanda gave no protest. Once aunt and niece headed off to Mary's house, Edna refilled Charlie's coffee mug. "Starling said you wanted to talk to me. I assume it's about Peppa's accident last night."

"It is," he said, taking a cell phone out of his jacket pocket. He studied the display, fiddled with the buttons, and finally handed it to Edna. "Can you identify this?"

Edna studied the photo for several seconds before looking at him with a frown. "It's pretty crumpled, but I'd guess it's a Christmas Rose. Lily Beck has some blooming in her garden."

"Clem Peppafitch was clutching that one in his hand."

Edna gave a slow nod. "He's been working for Lily, living above her garage. Did you know that?"

"Not before this morning. John Forrester showed up at the scene. Knows all about the Becks."

Edna was puzzled. "Who's John Forrester?"

"Detective. Retired last year, but he listens to a police scanner and shows up whenever something interests him. He was the initial lead on the Haverstrum case a couple years back, so when he heard the call this morning, he drove over. He's an okay guy. Doesn't get in the way. Knows a lot about who's who around town, so he's usually more useful than interfering."

She was still a little confused. "Okay, he knows

about the Becks, but how did he happen to connect Clem to them?"

Charlie thought for a minute, as if the question had just occurred to him, too. Then rather than answer her, he asked one of his own. "Do you know when Clem started working for Lily Beck?"

"Sometime last fall, according to what Lily told me. Tuck says about six months. She ran into him last November when she was at Lily's for a garden club meeting."

Charlie lifted a hand, palm up. "There you have it. Forrester must have seen him there. I hear John's been revisiting the Haverstrum case. He probably dropped by to talk to Lily and could have met Clem then."

"Isn't that some sort of harassment?" Edna mused. "Why would he be questionning Lily? Wasn't that case closed?"

Charlie took a sip of coffee, delaying a moment before shrugging. "I heard it was, but I wasn't here much at that time. Back then, I was spending most of my time tracking a burglary ring between here and Canada."

"You said Forrester was the *initial* lead on the case. What does that mean?"

Charlie thought for a few seconds, frowning. "The day after Haverstrum's body was found, John was sent to Washington for two weeks. I thought it strange at the time to pull him off a major investigation for training, but that's what happened. Someone else took over. John never was part of the team again, even when he got back."

"Don't you think it's even odder then that he's

looking into it now?"

Charlie shrugged as if it were no big deal. "Maybe because it was something he started but wasn't able to finish. Sounds like he thinks it shouldn't have been closed, or it might be his way of keeping busy these days."

Edna thought about Rosie's obvious frustration when she'd talked about the detective who seemed to be reopening her husband's case. More than just a way to occupy himself, Edna thought. She realized the way Rosie talked, John Forrester was obsessed. Shaking her head as she remembered her own vulnerability when she'd been treated as a suspect, Edna decided it was useless to continue speculating about the old detective's motives. She looked again at the Christmas Rose displayed on Charlie's phone and returned to their earlier conversation. "Since Clem was living there and working for Lily, it's a good bet this came from her garden. Is that what you came to find out this morning?"

Charlie nodded. "That and whatever else you might be able to tell me about the species. Is there something significant about the plant itself? I'm wondering why he was clutching it. It doesn't seem like the sort of cut flower you'd bring to your lady love, not like a single red rose or something." he said. The tight set to his jaw told Edna his remark was not meant as a joke.

She remained silent for a minute as she stared at the photo, not so much seeing the picture as trying to pull a vague detail from the back of her mind. "I know it's poisonous." She looked up to see Charlie watching her. "If I recall, there might be blisters around or inside his mouth." Mentioning the symptoms brought another foggy image to her mind, but before she could grab hold of it, Charlie interrupted the thought, shaking his head.

"I didn't notice anything like that. I think I would have if they'd been obvious. I'll ask the medical examiner if I don't see it in his report. We won't get that for a few days yet, I'm afraid." He paused briefly before going on. "Just how poisonous is this plant?"

Edna shrugged. She thought about Lettie's comment that her grandmother made "medicine" from the plant, but decided not to mention it until Charlie could tell her about the M.E.'s conclusions. She didn't want to muddy waters, if it weren't relevant to the case. Aloud, she said, "I remember bits and pieces, but I need to refresh my memory. I want to look over Mrs. Rabichek's journals again. How soon do you need to know?"

"Yesterday," Charlie answered with a grim smile.

She studied the detective as she thought about what Tuck had told her and tried to put it together with what he was asking. "How did Clem die? I thought you arrested Peppa for running him over with her car, but you're asking about the Christmas Rose. Are you thinking he might have been poisoned?"

"I'm not thinking anything at the moment. I'm just following up on whatever leaves a question in my mind. That flower in his hand, for instance …" Charlie paused to nod at the picture displayed on the phone she still held. "That is something we don't usually find on a corpse."

"So you don't actually know if Peppa killed him or not?" Edna was mostly thinking aloud and didn't like any of the implications, so far. "You've ruled out natural causes?"

Charlie shook his head and reached for his cell. "I didn't say that. What I said was, we won't know anything definite until we have the M.E.'s report."

"What about Peppa? Is she under arrest or not?"

"There's enough evidence, plus motive, to hold her, if they decide to. You know better than I do that Peppa held a lot of resentment against Clem. We're all trying to give her the benefit of the doubt and, until the results of the autopsy are in, I'm looking into whatever else I can find, but I'm not the lead on this. Whether she's booked or not isn't my decision." He held up the phone, redirecting her attention. "How much information do you think Mrs. Rabichek's journals will have about it?"

Edna shrugged. "I'll look and let you know." Sensing he was ready to leave, and remembering her promise to Tuck, she said hurriedly, "How's Peppa holding up?"

It was Charlie's turn to shrug. "I haven't spoken to her since last night when Detective King took her to the station for questioning, but I understand her lawyer was seeing the judge this morning. He's asking to have her released. Says we don't have enough evidence to hold her." Charlie snorted a laugh. "What do you want to bet the judge is one of her Saturday morning story kids?"

Edna laughed too, but as with Charlie, there was appreciation but not a lot of humor in it. "I'll call later today and see if there's anything I can do for her."

She saw Charlie to the door, extracting a promise from him that he'd keep her posted with whatever news he could reveal about the case, knowing he couldn't say much about an ongoing investigation. In turn, she told him she'd look at Mrs. Rabichek's journals as soon as possible and call him with whatever she found. As she closed the door, she wondered at the coincidence of another Beck being linked to a suspicious death. Could Clem's fatality be, in any way, connected to that of Lily's son-in-law? She shook her head to clear her mind. *The thought is too absurd.*

Chapter 10

Taking advantage of Starling and Amanda's absence after Charlie's departure, Edna went to her office and picked up the three volumes that comprised the journals Mrs. Rabichek had left when Edna and Albert purchased the house nearly two years before. Not remembering where she had found it before, she scanned the first book with no luck in finding any mention of the Christmas Rose. Two thirds of the way through the second tome, she found her reference.

To her surprise, the word that caught her eye first was *buttercup*. She read on, recalling more of the facts as she did so. *Christmas Rose--a perennial flowering plant in the buttercup family Ranunculaceae. Dark, leathery, pedate leaves. Stems 9 to 12 inches tall. Large flat white flowers on short stems. Blooms from midwinter to early spring. Difficult to grow*, Mrs. Rabichek had gone on to note. *Prefers moist alkaline soil, rich in humus.*

As was her custom, the elderly herbalist had noted medical uses in green ink. For the Christmas Rose, she had written *old days: used to treat paralysis, gout, insanity. More recent: toothache, earache, indigestion.*

Her color coding further consisted of warnings in red ink. *Highly toxic. Not recommended for human use. Poisonous substance is ranunculin. Acrid taste. Causes burning of eyes, mouth and throat.*

Antidotes would be listed in blue ink. There was no such entry for this section.

Not very pleasant, Edna thought, marking the page with a yellow sticky flag. She was about to pick up the phone to call Charlie with what she'd learned when she heard loud knocking on the front door. Followed by Benjamin, she went down the hall, wondering who would be calling, unannounced, at eleven o'clock on a Sunday morning.

Standing on the stoop was a stranger. He was a big man who looked to be about Edna's own age. An inch or two over six feet, he had a heavy paunch and sagging jowls beneath a bulbous nose. He wore his iron-gray hair in a military buzz cut. Mirrored sunglasses hid his eyes.

Instantly wary, Edna kept the screen door shut, relieved when she glanced down and reassured herself that she had locked it earlier, after Charlie left. "Yes?" she said, when the man said nothing. He seemed to be waiting for her to push the screen door open. "May I help you?"

"I want a word with you," he said. "May I come in?"

"Who are you? What do you want?"

"Name's John Forrester. I want to talk to you."

Edna instantly recognized the name of the retired detective Charlie had mentioned as the first lead on the Haverstrum investigation. Charlie had said he was a good guy. Perhaps it was Rosie's reaction to the detective that made Edna reluctant to unlock the screen and allow Forrester to enter. "I'm busy at the moment.

Tell me what you want."

"You've been asking questions about the Gregory Haverstrum case." He made the statement sound accusatory.

"Yes." Edna didn't follow her single-word response with "so what," but she might as well have from the scowl on Forrester's face.

"I've come to tell you to find something else to occupy your time. That investigation is none of your business."

"I beg your pardon?" Edna was taken aback by the man's abruptness.

"I think you heard me, Miz Davies. I said stop meddling."

Edna felt her cheeks start to warm as her temper rose. She fought to sound reasonable. "I understand the case is closed. Why would you consider any questions I have as interfering?"

He answered her question with another of his own. "Why did you tell Rosie Haverstrum she doesn't have to talk to me."

"I didn't exactly put it like that, but she doesn't, does she?" Edna said, confused as to why it would matter so much to this retired policeman. The case was closed and that should be the end of it, yet according to Rosie, John Forrester had begun to investigate again.

Edna took a step back in order to shut the door. She didn't like this man. Charlie might think well of his former colleague, but she didn't. The man was arrogant and bullying. No wonder Rosie got upset at the mere mention of the former detective.

As Edna closed the door, she heard him call out,

"No more amateur detecting or two-bit advice to Rosie Haverstrum. I'm warning you."

Heart racing, Edna stood with her back pressed against the door until she heard a car door slam and the sound of tires retreating around the broken shell driveway. She remained still for another minute or two, waiting for her heartbeat to slow. Looking down, she saw Benjamin staring at her. His head was tilted slightly and he seemed to be either curious or concerned or both. Whatever it was, she was distracted enough to relax a little and even smile as she bent to stroke his head. Her feeling of relief was quickly replaced by one of determination, as she headed to her office to call Charlie. Now, not only would she have information on the Christmas Rose, but she'd give him an earful about what she thought of his pal. She was standing by her desk, taking in deep breaths to calm herself further before reaching for the phone, when she heard Amanda's voice calling from the kitchen.

"I'm in here, sweetie," Edna called back, forcing John Forrester to the back of her mind. She would not let him spoil her last day's visit with her granddaughter. She sat and swiveled her chair in time to greet Amanda as the girl came bounding into the office, face flushed. Edna guessed Amanda had run across the yard from the neighboring house.

"Mary says it sounds like the ghost is riding a horse," the youngster said, flinging herself down onto the chair next to Edna's desk.

Benjamin, most likely alerted by the girl's voice, had vacated his favorite office chair seconds before Amanda sat. He ambled from the room with only the briefest, resentful glance over his shoulder, having deftly avoided being picked up by the youngster.

As Edna was enjoying these antics and taking in what Amanda had said, Starling appeared in the doorway and leaned a shoulder against the doorjamb, pushing her hands into the side pockets of her black woolen slacks.

"A horse?" Edna gave her daughter an amused, raised-eyebrow look while Amanda's attention was on the disappearing cat.

"That's right," Starling returned. "Mary's been researching South County history, practically back to the first settlers. She's now pretty certain that her rebel ghost must be reenacting Paul Revere's ride. A Rhode Island version of the ride, if there ever was such a thing," Starling added with a shrug. "She swears the noise sounds like hoof beats."

"We learned about Paul Revere in school," Amanda announced with some pride. "We're studying King Philip's War now." She frowned, adding, "I don't think 'King Philip' sounds much like an indian name."

"His real name was Metacomet," Edna explained. "The colonists just called him King Philip."

"Why?" Amanda demanded.

"Probably because they couldn't remember or pronounce his Wampanoag name."

"I wouldn't want strangers doing that to me," Amanda said, wrinkling her brow.

Changing the subject, Edna asked, "Did you know that King Philip hid from the settlers in the Great Swamp?"

Amanda nodded enthusiastically. "That's what my

teacher said."

"Do you know it's not far from here?" Starling asked.

Amanda's large brown eyes turned to her aunt as she slowly shook her head. "Where?"

"Know where Larkin Pond is?"

Amanda nodded. "That's where I go to Girl Scout camp."

Starling smiled at her niece. "That's the place. The Great Swamp is just down the road from Camp Hoffman. Wanna go see it? Should be a nice day for a walk. The wind's down and it'll be warmer away from the ocean."

The girl's eyes glowed with excitement. "Can I take pictures to show my teacher?"

"You bet."

Looking at the time on her computer screen, Edna broke in. "Let's have lunch and then take a ride over there, shall we?"

"Good idea. I'm hungry," Starling said. "How about you, Manda-Panda?"

The girl nodded, then looked skeptical. "What are we having?"

Edna laughed at her granddaughter's suspicion and thought she might have had enough seafood. "How about tomato soup and grilled cheese sandwiches?" she said, mentioning one of her children's favorite meals when they were young.

"Yeah," Amanda nearly shouted.

"Why don't you go help your aunt set the table, and I'll be there shortly," Edna said. "I've a call to make first." She then turned to Starling. "Do you have dinner plans with Charlie tonight?"

Starling shook her head. "He didn't mention anything. He's probably busy with Peppa's case, and he knows I have to drive back to Boston tonight."

"Tonight?" Edna was side-tracked for the moment. "I thought you weren't leaving until tomorrow morning." She felt a brief pang of sadness, missing her girls already.

"I changed my mind, especially when I thought of trying to get my niece up that early. Plus, if I leave tonight, I can avoid morning rush hour."

Surprisingly, Amanda didn't comment on her aunt's implied accusation. Edna thought the girl was probably happy that she wouldn't be rousted before dawn.

"You're probably right," Edna admitted reluctantly before picking up her earlier thought. "I need to call Charlie with some information. Since you don't have other plans, I'll see if he can join us this evening." Edna looked back at her granddaughter and smiled. "How would you like to make Auntie Starling's favorite meat loaf and mashed potatoes for supper?"

Again, the child nodded vigorously, jumped up from her chair and trailed Starling to the kitchen, while Edna picked up the phone to call Charlie and extend the invitation. When he accepted with enthusiasm, she gave him only the highlights of what she'd learned from Mrs. Rabichek's journal. He could read the page for himself. She also decided to save her temper and tell him about John Forrester's visit later that evening.

She had just pushed herself up from the chair to go to the kitchen when she had another thought. Turning back to the phone, she dialed Mary's number and asked her to join them for the afternoon's excursion and the evening's meal. Since Starling would be taking Amanda home after supper, Edna thought a small impromptu party would be fun for the child's last night.

"Pretty tragic what happened in the Great Swamp," Mary said, after learning where they were going. "Besides the warriors, all those Wampanoag women and children were killed by the colonial militia." She paused for a second or two before asking, "Think the old fort site is haunted?"

"I think you've got ghosts on the brain." Edna laughed.

"Maybe so. Thanks, but I'll skip the walk. I need sleep. Can't get much at night, so I'm taking a nap this afternoon. I'll have dinner with you, though."

"Good. Why don't you come over around five for drinks first."

Chapter 11

The trip to the Great Swamp was a success. There was very little wind blowing in amongst the trees and, although the broad path was covered with several inches of snow, it was fresh and clean. Theirs were the only footprints.

Amanda and Starling took many photos--Amanda with a small digital and Starling with a larger, more professional camera. Although the site was mostly a nature walk with nothing that looked like ruins or an abandoned village, they did get some shots of the rough-cut granite monument and memorial plaque that had been placed there by the Rhode Island Society of Colonial Wars. On the way back to the car, Edna was thrilled to see a Cedar Waxwing with its brown, gray and yellow plumage. She was about to call it to the others' attention when she noticed they had spotted it too. With quiet joy, Edna watched Starling give instructions to her niece.

Bending so her mouth was close to Amanda's ear, Starling spoke in a low voice. "See the bird in that bush with the red berries. Move really slowly so you don't scare him, but zoom in and see if you can get a shot."

Amanda obeyed. It might have been a movement or a sound that frightened the bird away just as she took the picture. With a look of dismay, she turned to Starling and shrugged in exaggerated frustration.

"No, wait," Starling encouraged. "Look at your display. I think you caught him."

Dutifully, Amanda examined the back of the camera as she twisted her body to cast a shadow onto the small screen. As soon as her eyes lit up, Edna knew Starling had been right.

With a grin spreading from ear to ear, the girl showed first Starling, then Edna, a nearly perfectly framed picture of the Cedar Waxwing with a red berry in his beak and wings just lifting in flight.

"Wow. Terrific shot," Starling said, pulling her niece into a one-armed hug.

Nothing more exciting happened, but for Edna, the afternoon went all too quickly, and they returned home barely in time to get ready for their supper guests. As usual, Mary arrived early. She looked more rested than she had in the last few days and admitted to having had a good two-hour nap. Shortly after five, Charlie showed up with a bouquet of flowers that he'd obviously bought at the grocery store in town.

"Pretty flowers for a pretty girl," he said, handing the spray to Amanda with a stately bow.

Accepting them, Amanda giggled and blushed.

Starling bent to stage-whisper in her ear, "Say 'thank you, kind sir' and curtsey."

Amanda obeyed with more giggles and accompanying good-humored laughs from her audience.

Starling encouraged Amanda to show her photographs to Mary and Charlie while Edna found a vase for the flowers and made an arrangement for the middle of the dining room table. Knowing her granddaughter would have a great time showing them off to her family and friends, she told Amanda that she was to take the flowers home, container and all.

Drinks and appetizers were followed by the meat loaf Amanda made with only a small amount of guidance from Edna. It was a favorite family recipe, served with buttery mashed potatoes. Starling's contribution was a green salad, and Mary's offering was homemade chocolate and walnut brownies. Edna brewed tea.

After dinner, Edna was loading the dishwasher. "Would you like to phone Lettie that you're leaving?" she asked her granddaughter as Amanda handed her plates and glasses from the table.

The girl shook her head. "I'll see her when I get home."

Edna frowned. "I don't understand. If she's staying with her grandmother, how are you going to see her?"

"She's not."

Edna shook her head to see if maybe she could clear away the cobwebs and make some sense of the remark. After a brief pause, she gave up. "Not what?" she asked.

Having gone back to the table to clear away cups and saucers, Amanda didn't answer until she was back at Edna's side. "Not at her grandmother's," the girl said as if it were obvious or as if Edna should have known. "She texted me this morning on Auntie Starling's phone to say she was going home with her mother."

Odd behavior, thought Edna, wondering briefly why Rosie had changed her mind about leaving Lettie with Lily. Had Rosie thought Amanda accompanying Lettie would provide safety in numbers? Was the tension between Rosie and Lily at the root of this change in plans? Edna dismissed these ideas almost as soon as they popped into her head. She couldn't imagine Rosie putting her daughter in the middle of a spat with her mother. Remembering the constant texting, Edna was certain Rosie simply missed her daughter and wanted her home.

The evening passed as fast as the afternoon had and, before she knew it, Edna's daughter and granddaughter were packing their suitcases into Starling's ancient blue Toyota Celica and hugging her goodbye.

Edna, Charlie and Mary returned to the living room. Attracted by the warmth of a low fire in the grate, Benjamin went to curl up in his bed by the hearth. Edna felt a bittersweet sadness, as she always did when members of her family drove off after a visit. An image of her granddaughter's face, flushed with happiness as she settled into the car with her vase of flowers, assured Edna that it had indeed been a special evening for the girl.

"How's that ghost of yours?" Charlie's voice brought Edna's attention back to her present company. The detective was speaking to Mary as he sank into one corner of the sofa while she took the other.

"Louder than ever," Mary complained. "I hear him soon's I turn off the late news every night. Can't get to sleep while he's galloping back and forth over my head."

"What's happening with Peppa's case?" Edna asked Charlie before the conversation deteriorated into another discussion of Mary's mythical ghost. *Colonial rebel on horseback, indeed*, she thought with a mental shrug before another idea popped into her head. *I wonder what causes it to pick that particular time, and with such regularity.* She would have to ask Mary about it further, but at the moment, she wanted to know about her retired librarian friend.

"I'm still stymied by that flower Clem was clutching," Charlie said, rubbing one hand through his brown curls.

"That reminds me," Edna said, rising to fetch Mrs. Rabichek's journal from her office. Returning, she handed Charlie the volume she'd flagged for the Christmas Rose entry.

"Have you asked Peppa?" she said, resuming her seat. "Maybe it was a peace offering. Perhaps that particular plant had some special meaning for the Peppafitches when she and Clem were married."

Charlie shook his head in answer to her question. Opening to the marked page, he read in silence for a minute or two before closing the book and laying it on the sofa between Mary and himself. "Doesn't tell me much more than when we talked this morning about possible blistering near his mouth, except for the specific poison," he said, bending forward to pull a notebook and pen from a back pocket in his slacks. He wrote briefly, then looked over at Edna as he replaced the notebook and sat back. "I'll tell the M.E.'s office about ranunculin, but I'd bet they're already on top of it."

"Has Peppa gone home?" Edna asked, still concerned for her friend. "I promised Tuck I'd try to smooth the waters between the two of them. I also want to take one of my casseroles to Peppa. She probably isn't in much of a mood to cook for herself."

"She left with her lawyer late this afternoon," Charlie said.

"Tuck said she's been charged with murder. Can that be right, if you haven't even gotten autopsy results back yet?"

Charlie shook his head. "Peggy King took her to the station to answer questions. She couldn't be interviewed at home because we needed to process the scene without people tramping up and down the driveway."

"Did Peppa mind very much … being taken away, I mean?"

Charlie laughed. "I doubt it. Ask me, I'd say she wanted to see how many of our personnel she'd recognize. You know how she loves attention from her Saturday morning kids."

Edna nodded. Knowing Peppa, Charlie was right. "I'll phone her first thing in the morning."

"Wanna stay over with me tonight?" Mary turned to look at Edna. She had been staring into the fire, seeming to pay little attention to the conversation going on between Edna and Charlie.

"I'm sorry," Edna said with a shake of her head. "I'm too tired tonight, and I've a lot on my mind right now." *And not just about Peppa*, Edna thought as the memory of John Forrester's visit popped into her head. Looking disappointed but not defeated, Mary picked up the journal on the seat next to her. Unlike her normally curious self, she seemed to tune out the conversation once again as Edna told Charlie about Forrester showing up on her doorstep.

"What did he want?" Charlie had turned to study

the small log fire and appeared to be only partially interested in hearing about the retired detective.

"He threatened me."

"What?" Charlie's head jerked back to glare at her, eyes widening in surprise before his face relaxed into a smile of incredulity. "You must have misunderstood. John wouldn't threaten you. Fact is, I can't imagine Gentleman John intimidating anyone."

"I did not misunderstand." Edna was adamant. "He told me in no uncertain terms that I was to stop asking questions about Gregory Haverstrum's death *or else*."

"Why *are* you so interested in that old case?"

"Because his wife is still living with suspicion hanging over her head, and that same doubt is having its effect on their daughter. That same daughter is Amanda's new best friend."

Understanding sparked in Charlie's eyes, but he asked anyway, "Just like when Tom was poisoned and the town's people thought you did it. Is that what's going on in your head?"

Edna nodded, not trusting herself to speak as she thought of her old handyman and friend. Tom had been Mary's friend, too, since their high school days. She perked up at his name. Putting the book back down on the settee, she looked from Charlie to Edna. "I don't think Tom would haunt my attic." Then, after a few seconds' pause during which two pairs of eyes stared at her, she added, "Do you?"

Chapter 12

Monday morning, Edna woke early, feeling rested and refreshed. The sky was still dark as she lay in bed, planning her day, but the forecast was for sunshine and warmer temperatures. She'd phone Albert and see how the fishing trip was going. She'd thought about calling him the previous evening after Charlie and Mary left, but it had been nearly ten o'clock and, after the day's events, she'd been too tired both mentally and physically. She'd merely trudged up the stairs and fallen into a deep sleep.

She must call Peppa, too. Edna wondered how her friend was feeling about her ex-husband. In the year and a half Edna had known the woman, Peppa had vaguely referred to her marriage only twice, and each time had been clouded with anger or disgust. The memory of Peppa's scornful remarks about Clem prompted Edna to get out of bed, shower and dress. She knew from past experience that the only way to rid her mind of unpleasant musings was to get busy. As a result, shortly after six, she was in the kitchen making breakfast.

By seven, she had finished a plate of scrambled eggs and oatmeal muffins, completed the daily crossword puzzle and swallowed the last of her second cup of coffee. Still too early to phone either Albert or Peppa, she went to her office and sat at the computer.

After checking for messages, she decided to do more research into the Haverstrum and Beck families.

Wanting more background information, she decided to research Gregory Havstrum's mistresses. She searched first for Farren McCree. The image that appeared was of a strikingly pretty woman. Her red-gold hair was shoulder length and waved attractively around her face. Above high cheek bones, her deep blue eyes were slightly almond shaped. This was the woman with whom Gregory betrayed his wife, then threw over for a teenager. Edna wondered what Bobbi Callahan must be like. She couldn't help feeling that Haverstrum had either been very shallow or extremely insecure not only to carry on an affair while he was married to a woman as lovely as Rosie, but then to toss aside another attractive, mature woman for someone barely out of high school. Realizing she was getting side-tracked, Edna forced her thoughts back to Farren McCree.

The woman had been several years older than her married lover. She also claimed to be Rosie's best friend, but had carried on an affair with that friend's husband, or so the news reporters alleged. Both wife and mistress were employed at the same place at the time of Gregory's death. Edna wondered if Farren still worked at the local greenhouse.

Taking a small notebook and pen from her top desk drawer, Edna wrote down the shop's name and address. She'd visit the place today, she thought, going to the business web site to find that they would be open from ten until four. At the nursery, she would use the excuse that she needed to decide on which annuals to plant in the back patio pots this spring. She wouldn't need to buy, she'd only be looking for future consideration. She would ask for Farren, claiming that a friend had recommend the shop and the woman. If Farren had left the company's employ, certainly someone would know where she had gone, and Edna would simply have more work to do to track Farren down.

Edna wondered what she could say to the woman or if Farren would talk to her at all about something that had taken place two years ago. The thought brought John Forrester's face to mind, and Edna shuddered as she speculated on whether or not he was currently hounding Farren and Bobbi as well as Rosie and Lily.

Edna next searched for Bobbi Callahan. According to the news reports, Haverstrum had hired the young woman as a general office assistant. Edna entered Bobbi's name into the computer's search box and found a LinkedIn page. Again Gregory had chosen a woman who would turn heads. With platinum blonde hair, Bobbi resembled Rosie more than Farren, but her eyes were brown instead of the deep blue of Gregory's other women. According to the brief background summary that the young woman had posted, Edna read that now, at age twenty-one, Bobbi would receive a bachelor's degree in May and, in the fall, would begin her first full-time teaching job at a nearby elementary school.

Edna also knew from online reports that Bobbi had applied for the job with Haverstrum because of the flexible hours which allowed her to work around her sophomore class schedule. Reports further revealed that although Duke Callahan was a wealthy man, he wanted to instill a sense of responsibility and accomplishment in his daughter, and so encouraged her to earn anything over and above the college tuition that he provided. As an assistant, Bobbi performed tasks from opening the mail, fielding phone calls and typing up contracts to picking up Gregory's dry cleaning. "Go-fer," Edna muttered as she wondered if Bobbi had been enamored of the man who was at least fifteen years her senior, if she was flattered by his attentions, or if she played up to the letch in order to keep a convenient and well-paying job.

Eight chimes from the grandfather clock brought Edna out of the depths of those meanderings. Since she had an address with which she could begin looking for Farren, she'd go to the nursery first. If she found the woman, Edna would simply play her approach by ear. Enough time had been spent pondering the anticipated meeting when she knew absolutely nothing about Farren's personality. Edna decided she needed to get on with her day and stop dwelling on unknowns. Picking up the phone, she dialed Albert's cell number.

"Have I caught you at a bad time?" she asked when he answered on the fifth ring.

"No, sweetheart. I'm just sitting here reading the morning paper. How are you?"

"I'm fine. How about you? How's your knee?" she asked, wondering if pain or stiffness were the reason he'd taken so long to take her call, if indeed he'd simply been sitting and reading the paper.

"Still attached."

"Are you walking without the cane?" She ignored his attempt at humor and evasion.

"Not yet, but I'm getting there. Feelin' stronger every day."

She wouldn't push him for more information at the moment, realizing she'd get better answers from Matthew when she spoke with her son. Changing the subject, she said, "Who's winning the bets?"

He gave a short bark of laughter. "I was ahead in the category for most fish for the week, but Roger inched me out last thing yesterday. He's now ahead by one. Matthew's leading in size for the week, but I caught the biggest marlin of the day yesterday, so didn't have to cook dinner or wash dishes last night."

"Sounds like you've added to your categories."

"Sort of. We decided on a daily contest as well as our original end-of-the-trip total. Winners for the day get waited on that evening. Leaves at least two to make drinks, cook and clean up." He chuckled. "Ken's become pretty good at grilling."

"What are your plans for today?" she asked, entertained by the thought of the men and their friendly betting. Knowing Ken, she guessed her son-in-law's father was enjoying the role of head chef and wondered with some amusement if he were purposely losing the wagers.

"We're relaxing this morning. Captain Patrick has some business in town, so we're not heading out 'til after lunch."

"Are the boys there?" she said, thinking to say hello to her son and son-in-law.

"Nope. I'm alone at the moment. Matthew and Roger went down to walk the beach and Ken's out buying groceries."

Edna wondered again why Albert had chosen to stay in and was more determined than ever to get a report on his knee from her son. She thought briefly of dialing Matthew's number when she hung up from Albert, but their son might have left his cell in the condo. If it rang and Albert answered, she'd be caught, she thought with a grimace. She knew her husband well enough to know that he wouldn't appreciate her making a fuss over his condition.

Giving up on the idea, she placed a call to Peppa, but the phone went unanswered. Edna next dialed Tuck.

"Is Peppa with you?" Edna asked after the preliminary greetings were over.

"No. Why?"

"I just tried calling her, but there was no answer."

"My guess is she's avoiding reporters. I've been lying low myself, but the whole town probably knows by now that she ran over Clem with that old Mercedes of hers. I imagine the papers are trying to hound her for a story."

"Is she speaking to you yet?" Edna mentally crossed her fingers, hoping for a positive reply, but her heart sank with Tuck's next words.

"Don't know. She hasn't phoned me, though. I thought about driving over to her house, but I don't think I could stand to have her slam the door in my face. I'm waiting for you to give me the all clear," Tuck said, sounding sheepish.

Edna quietly sighed with resignation. She didn't like being put in the middle of someone else's quarrel, but she also didn't want those two to be at odds. They'd been best friends far too long. "No promises, but I'll see what I can do."

After ending the call with Tuck, Edna tried once

more to reach Peppa. Surely, she'd have caller ID and know it was Edna who was phoning, but still there was no pick-up. Beginning to feel some concern, Edna decided to visit Peppa with the pretext of taking a casserole to her. She probably wouldn't be in the mood to cook for herself. If Peppa wasn't answering her phone, she probably wasn't going to the grocery store, either.

It was Edna's practice to keep at least one or two frozen meals on hand for emergencies, easily done by doubling a recipe she'd be making for dinner and freezing half. This morning, she selected a chicken divan dish. Made with broccoli and lots of cheese in the basic white sauce, the result was both healthy and comforting. She was about to shut the freezer door, when she spotted a container of clam chowder and pulled that out, too. As she loaded a tote bag with the frozen food and went to the closet for her coat, she wondered again why Peppa wouldn't be answering calls from friends. Edna suddenly felt a shiver run down her spine as she thought about the retired librarian. What must she be thinking about the death of the man whom she'd once loved and respected enough to marry? Would she be distressed enough to harm herself?

Chapter 13

When Edna reached Peppa's house, all was quiet. The driveway was no longer cordoned off with crime scene tape, so she was able to pull up and park in front of the garage. There had obviously been activity in the yard. What remained of the snow had been churned into mud with bits of grass mixed in. Many boots had been tramping around the yard, littering dirt up and down the driveway, but all emergency vehicles were gone now. She was relieved also to find no reporters or TV vans crowding the narrow, residential street.

Peppa's Mercedes was nowhere in sight, but Edna couldn't see into the garage. She wondered if the car were there or if it had been towed away for forensic examination. At the front door, she rang the bell, waited, knocked and waited another half minute before pressing the button again. More forcefully this time, as if additional strength could somehow prompt her friend to answer.

As she waited on the stoop, Edna wondered if Peppa might be back at the police station for more questioning. Or had she gone to visit Tuck? Edna was about to give up and head back to her car when she became aware of barking coming from the backyard and decided to investigate. She brightened somewhat at the sound. Peppa must have been home at some point if

Rufus was there, Edna thought, rounding the corner of the house. Or maybe Tuck had brought the dog back and left him in the yard, once she'd learned that Peppa wouldn't be spending the night in jail. As Edna reached the wooden gate, she couldn't see over the six-foot fence, but she heard the Rottweiler on the other side of the cedar slats.

"Hey, Rufus," she called over the racket, reaching for the latch. "It's me, fella." When his barking changed to a whine of expectation, she pushed through the gate, nudging the canine backwards. Rubbing his head and scratching his ears as his tail wagged his entire back end, she spoke gently to him. "There's a good dog. Where's your mistress?" Edna chatted and petted and made her way slowly along the side of the house to the back deck, intending to look through the window into the kitchen. She never made it that far.

Passing the corner of the house and moving alongside the railing, she saw what looked like a quilt draped over a pile of blankets and clothing on a lawn chair in the middle of the redwood deck. Mounting the steps, she was startled by a slight motion beneath the mound which drew her attention to a red stocking cap. Between the blanket and hat, only eyes, nose and mouth could be seen. Her first instinct was to apologize and turn around to leave the way she came when the eyes flicked again in her direction. Peppa's gray-blue eyes.

She took a steadying breath, trying to still her hammering heart. "Hey, Peppa. What're you doing out here?"

"Walkin' the dog" came the curt reply from the chair. Only Peppa's lips moved.

"Are you cold?" The morning air was crisp and cool. The temperature was probably in the low to mid forties, Edna estimated. Not cold enough to warrant the heavy wrappings with which Peppa had bundled herself.

The old librarian's head slowly moved from side to side, but she kept her eyes fixed on the backyard.

"How long have you been sitting here?"

Peppa shrugged, or at least that's how it looked to Edna who noticed only a slight shifting of the quilt.

"When you didn't answer the door, I thought something might have happened to you," Edna said, explaining why she had invaded the woman's privacy. Peppa remained silent and motionless, almost as if she hadn't heard.

Edna tried another tack. She held up the tote bag. "I brought a casserole and some of my world-famous chowda," she said, trying to get a laugh out of Peppa, or a smile, at least. When that didn't work, she gave in to an intuition. "Have you had anything to eat since yesterday morning?"

After a brief pause, Peppa once again swiveled her head from side to side, but kept her eyes straight ahead. "Not hungry," she muttered.

"Have you spoken to anyone?" Edna asked, adding "besides Rufus?" as the dog went to stand beside his owner. She, in turn, slid a hand from beneath the quilt to stroke his head.

Either the dog or the motion seemed to bring Peppa out of her catatonic state, and she finally turned her gaze on Edna who, by now, was sitting on a low, white metal table.

Deciding to take the action as a positive sign, Edna

stood and held out a hand. "Come inside, Peppa," she encouraged. "Let me make you a nice hot cup of tea and maybe some toast. When you've had something to eat, we should talk."

Peppa stared up at Edna for nearly half a minute before she spread wide the blankets and raised a hand for Edna to help her up. Under the bedding, she wore a woolen coat, the red of which matched her cap. Her feet were clad in gray Mukluks.

Following her friend into the house, Edna realized Peppa was suffering from emotional shock. One thing she must do is talk about her experience and feelings, whether to Edna or better yet, to her best friend in the world. Edna decided to call Tuck and get the two friends speaking again as soon as possible.

After shedding coats and hats and leaving them on the coat tree inside the back door, the two women moved to the kitchen where Edna gently guided Peppa to a chair at the table while she herself set the kettle on to boil. She put the clam chowder and the chicken casserole into the fridge before opening the milk carton to smell that it was fresh. Eyeing a partial carton of eggs next to a wedge of cheddar, she decided to make a cheese omelet. Peppa might eat if food were placed in front of her.

Having prepared and set the small meal before Peppa, Edna took the chair on the opposite side of the table with her own mug of tea. She sat quietly while Peppa broke off a bit of buttered toast and fed it to Rufus. She then commanded the dog to lie down, before picking up her fork and slowly beginning to eat. After the first few bites, she glanced up at Edna and nodded.

"Thank you. Guess I needed this."

"Do you want to talk?" Edna asked, resting her forearms on the table as she held the warm mug between her hands.

Peppa chewed, swallowed and shrugged. "Don't know what to say."

Edna thought about the lean, weathered man she'd met and how kind he'd been. "I met Clem recently," she said, hoping to spark some sort of conversation. She didn't know what she expected to learn, but knew Peppa needed a sounding board. Edna suspected, if not pushed, her friend would bottle her emotions inside where they would fester.

Peppa stopped eating with the fork halfway to her mouth. Lowering the utensil, she frowned at Edna. "Where?"

"Lily Beck's place. Last Friday afternoon. Did you know he was working for her, living above the garage?"

"Didn't know. Tuck knew, though."

Edna hadn't meant to get drawn in to their quarrel but she had, first by Tuck and now by Peppa. "Tuck told me that she promised Clem to keep his secret. She said he was meaning to contact you, but in his own time, when he was ready."

After a moment's hesitation, Peppa nodded as if that made sense. "Sounds like something he'd do … she, too, I suppose," Peppa said and resumed eating.

When she made no further attempt to talk and merely concentrated on the food, Edna explained how she'd driven her granddaughter and a friend down from Warwick for a visit. Mainly to fill the silence, she mentioned the coincidence that Amanda's friend was

Lily's granddaughter and how, when Edna had arrived at the Beck house, Clem had been in the driveway, polishing a car. Edna also relayed how rude Lily had seemed to him, but how tolerant and unruffled he had remained. Edna didn't know how Peppa felt about her ex-husband, especially now that he was dead, so other than the one observation of Lily's behavior, she refrained from giving any other opinion. She ended her tale with Clem's patching the tire.

Peppa nodded again, put down her fork, and pushed the empty plate aside. Picking up the tea mug, she took a slow sip of her drink. "He was always good at fixin' things."

"If you don't mind my asking, what happened between you two?" Edna still hoped she could get Peppa to talk and shake her out of a lethargy that was not at all like the gregarious woman Edna had come to know.

"Booze." Peppa nearly spat the word. "More'n thirty years married when my husband decides to become an alcoholic."

"Certainly, you don't think it was a *decision* on his part?" Edna couldn't keep the surprise or disbelief from her tone. The ignorance in Peppa's condemnation disturbed Edna.

"Of course it wasn't a decision to become addicted to alcohol, but it *was* his decision to let it ruin himself, his job and our marriage." Peppa spoke harshly. "And don't expect me to change my mind or apologize for hanging onto my anger. For five years, I watched that man transform himself from a popular professor, adored by every one of his botany students, into a pathetic street bum. I put him to bed most nights when he could hardly stand, never mind speak. When he could talk, I listened to his lies and empty promises. The day after he nearly killed an entire family, totaling his car in the process, I told him to get out and called a divorce lawyer."

Edna didn't know what to say. How do you respond to such memories or the anger, she wondered, and didn't even try. Instead, she changed the subject. "What happened Saturday night? Can you tell me about it?"

Peppa seemed to be caught off balance by the questions. Mentally, she was probably still back in the past and steaming with renewed resentment. It took several seconds for her to say, "Don't know." She squinted at Edna over the mug in her hands before setting it aside next to her empty plate. With a suddenness that made Edna jump and Rufus leap up, Peppa banged the flat of her hand on the table. "What was that fool doing lying across my driveway?" Her face was red with rage, and she hardly seemed to notice Rufus push his muzzle into her lap, but as she began to stroke the massive head, she also began to calm down. "I thought he'd done his worst to me years ago, but it seems he had one more card to play." Tears had sprung to the old librarian's eyes and she hung her head for a minute.

Edna remained silent, too, not knowing what to say to Peppa's outburst or how to assuage her ... what? What were the woman's emotions? They seemed a mix of fury, guilt, remorse. Perhaps a long-lost love was in there, too, somewhere.

After a few minutes of petting the Rottweiler, Peppa looked up and seemed to shake herself out of her blue funk, at least partially. "What have you heard? What're people saying?"

"I don't know. You should ask Tuck, if you want the local gossip. Her ear's closer to the ground than mine." Pausing briefly to consider if her question would upset Peppa again, Edna decided the woman needed to get her emotions out. "Speaking of Tuck, when she told me that she ran into Clem last fall at Lily's, I assumed he came back to town in order to see you again. Do you know why he hadn't contacted you up to now?"

"Haven't a clue," Peppa responded more quietly than Edna expected. "I can only guess that he wanted to establish himself, set himself up so I wouldn't think he expected to walk right back into my life. He never was one to rush. Always took his time thinkin' things over, plannin' out each and every step."

"Do you know why he was bringing you the Christmas Rose?"

Peppa shook her head. "He wasn't exactly bringing me flowers. I understand he had the blossom crushed in a tight fist."

"Does the plant have special significance for you?"

Again, Peppa shook her head. "Can't think of what it would be. The only thing 'Christmas' means to us is that it was the day he put a father, mother and baby in the hospital. I told him I was filing for divorce and kicked him out that day. I doubt he'd want to commemorate *that*."

Chapter 14

Peppa seemed to sink back into herself after telling the story of her last battle with Clem. Shortly thereafter, she excused herself, saying she wanted to change her clothes and wash up a bit. "Stay if you want, but I don't know why you would," she said before leaving the room. She was beginning to sound like her old self.

As soon as she was out of earshot, Edna went to the back door where she pulled the cell phone out of her coat pocket and dialed Tuck's number. Her friend must have been waiting for a call because she picked up on the first ring.

"You need to get over here," Edna said, after briefly explaining how she'd discovered Peppa on the back deck. "I think the dam has started to crack, but you must press her to keep talking. She can't keep all this hurt and hatred bottled up on top of the guilt she's probably feeling."

Tuck rang the bell twenty minutes later. Edna opened the door at the same time Peppa came downstairs and stopped on the bottom step. She frowned at Tuck who looked anxiously back. After half a minute of silence that seemed like half an hour to Edna, Peppa moved off the staircase and opened her arms. Tuck rushed to accept the hug, and Edna released the breath she hadn't realized she'd been holding. Her intuition was reaffirmed. The friendship between Peppa and Tuck was too strong not to survive small bumps in the road.

Once the ice broke and the two women began to talk, Edna didn't stay much longer. She'd done enough and was happy with the outcome. Before she'd even left the neighborhood, her thoughts turned to two young girls. She smiled at memories of the past few days spent with Amanda. The youngster was so full of energy and enthusiasm. Edna thought with a pang of nostalgia that all too soon the little girl would be a young woman, and Edna wouldn't see as much of her as other interests and activities occupied more of her granddaughter's time. Edna had already experienced this coming-of-age with her older grandchildren, but the natural-enough phenomenon still tugged at her heart.

She pushed thoughts of Amanda aside and replaced them with images of Lettie. The girl had seemed to enjoy their outing around the South County coast. She'd even laughed and chattered away happily with Amanda. According to Lettie's mother, that wasn't normal behavior for the girl. *But it should be*, Edna thought, feeling anger roil her insides. She'd felt the sting of suspicion and gossip herself, and it had bothered her as a mature adult. What must a nine-year-old child be feeling when she senses the contempt or sees suspicion in the eyes of strangers, let alone her classmates?

Stopped at a traffic light, Edna's attention was drawn to a man stepping out of a nearby florist's shop with a bouquet of red roses in his hand and a broad grin on his face. *Valentine's Day present*, she thought and slowly began to feel her fury dissipate. The sight of the flowers, however, caused her thoughts to switch to

Rosie and her friend-turned-traitor Farren McCree.

Edna glanced at the time on her dashboard. According to the web site she'd found as she'd dug around the Haverstrum case, the nursery where Farren McCree worked at the time of Gregory's death opened at ten during winter months. It was also not far away. Edna put on her turn signal as the light changed to green, made a left-hand turn and headed for the garden center. If she could find Farren, the woman might provide insights into her relationships--both with Rosie and with Gregory--that the news reports didn't provide … that is, if Edna could get her to talk at all about what happened two years ago.

The nursery was located in a rural neighborhood with off-road parking for about a dozen cars. Immediately inside double sliding doors was an area holding shopping carts and trolleys. Beyond that, another set of automatic doors opened into a temperate, humid area with a service desk to the right and check-out registers on the left. Ahead were free-standing displays holding a variety of gardening implements, gloves, books, pots and assorted other tools of the trade. Edna could tell by the high ceiling of translucent plastic that, behind the racks, the building stretched back for a considerable distance.

A pleasant-looking, sixty-something woman sat behind the low service counter which appeared to double as her work space with a computer, phone and stacks of paper. At Edna's inquiry, she said, "Yes. Miz McCree is one of our landscape designers. Would you like to speak with her? I can see if she's available."

Edna assented, and the woman promptly picked up

the receiver, pressed a button and paged Farren McCree to reception for customer assistance.

While she waited, Edna wandered over to look behind the displays. The nursery was long but not wide. Four rows of narrow tables running perpendicular to the entrance were filled with plants. The rear of the area looked to be a closed-off greenhouse, while off to her right was an open space filled with bags of soil, peat, mulch and shelves of planters and pots, decorative and utilitarian.

"Did you want to see me?" came a low-pitched, sultry voice from behind her.

Edna spun to look into the deep blue eyes of a strawberry-blonde beauty of medium height. Dressed in navy slacks and pink blouse with frills at the collar and cuffs, Farren McCree looked more like an office worker than a garden-center employee. She held out a business card and, as Edna took it, Farren introduced herself, adding. "How may I help you?"

Having been surprised by the sudden appearance of the woman, Edna had to think fast, wondering if she should come straight to the point or pretend to be a customer who needed professional advice. She decided if Farren made the slightest inquiry, she would soon find out that Edna was a member of the locally prestigious Greenthumbs garden society. Remembering the occasional flyers she received in the mail, Edna guessed the nursery had a list of club members. She decided honesty would get her into the least amount of trouble.

"To be truthful, I'm here to ask about Rosie Beck. I guess you knew her by her married name. Rosie Haverstrum?" She spoke the name as a question.

Farren looked startled for an instant before her eyes took on a hard glint that almost immediately turned neutral. "Who are you?"

"A friend. Rosie recently moved to my son's neighborhood. Her daughter and my granddaughter are school chums."

When Edna didn't offer more explanation, Farren shook her head as if confused. "I haven't spoken to Rosie for almost two years." Her face softened slightly as she said, "And Lettie. She must be, what, about ten now."

"Nine," Edna corrected and wondered if Farren had befriended her lover's daughter. She tucked the thought to the back of her mind for a later discussion.

Farren frowned. "Why would you ask me about them? Obviously, you've seen them more recently than I have."

A young couple pushing a cart came toward them, behind Farren. Edna took the woman by the forearm to move her out of the path, then looked around. "Is there a place where we can sit and talk?"

"I don't know what we have to talk about."

"Rosie's daughter is having trouble in school because of the uncertainty surrounding her father's death and her mother's notoriety. One of the reasons they moved to my son's neighborhood from where they'd been living is because people still suspect Rosie as having played a part in her husband's death. The children of these cynics seem to be taking it out on Lettie, as well."

"Sorry to hear that, but I don't see what it has to do with me." Farren shrugged but her eyes were no longer fixed on Edna's. She gazed around the room as if she were on an inspection tour.

"I'm trying to get a more complete picture of what went on at the time Gregory Haverstrum died, so I might be able to find a way to help Lettie." She took a step to her left, purposely placing herself in Farren's line of sight. If the woman worked in a nursery, she must have something of a nurturing personality, Edna guessed. She wasn't about to explain to this stranger that Edna's own experience, plus concern for a granddaughter, also played a large part in motivating her to hunt for the truth.

Farren's gaze returned to Edna's face and a frown creased her forehead. "Lettie? She was a sweet child. Why would anyone want to pick on her?"

The question seemed redundant, but Edna thought Farren just might be sympathetic toward the girl. "I'll be happy to tell you, but not in the middle of this store. Isn't there somewhere quieter where we can talk?"

Farren shrugged again, hesitated, then looked at her watch. "There's a little diner in the next block where we can get a cup of coffee. Why don't you meet me there? I can spare about thirty minutes, but then I'm meeting a client."

"Half an hour should be fine," Edna said, hoping it would be and, within that amount of time, Farren McCree could shed more light on what happened two years ago.

When they had settled into a booth at the Harborside Café and given their waitress an order for two coffees, Farren sat sullenly. She stared around the nearly empty room and appeared to regret her decision to meet with Edna. Hoping to put the woman at ease and get her to talk, Edna decided to ask Farren about herself. "How long have you worked at the garden center? You're a landscape architect, is that correct?"

"Designer. Architect. Pretty much the same thing," Farren said, concentrating on spreading a paper napkin across her lap.

Edna knew that an architect was licensed, and typically had more education and experience than a designer. She'd thrown out the title as a test of Farren's integrity. The woman had failed, which meant that Edna had just learned that she'd need to take the conversation with a grain of salt where the woman's ego was concerned.

"How long have you worked for the nursery?" Edna repeated her previous question.

"Six years this coming June."

"Was Rosie employed there at the time, or was she hired after you?"

Farren shook her head, finally looking directly at Edna. "She'd been employed almost two years when her husband died. After his body was found, she never did come back to work." Farren then sighed deeply, as if resigned to explaining the past. "I met the Haverstrums when Gregory hired me to plan their yard." Edna thought Farren would stop there, but she continued after only a brief pause. "They'd lived in the house for a few years, but had never sought professional advice. When Gregory's business began to take off, he decided to treat his top clients to a catered lawn party. For that reason, he wanted the yard designed by an expert. I understand, prior to that, his mother-in-law advised Rosie on what to do with the backyard."

Edna winced in mock horror. "Knowing the pride Lily Beck took in her own gardens, I doubt that hiring you would have gone over well with her."

"You're right on that count." Farren chuckled and rolled her eyes. "Fortunately, I don't think she resented me half as much as she did Gregory, though. He told me that she criticized the landscaping every time she came to the house. Which," Farren added with a grin, "was considerably more often than before the work began. I guess she made his life miserable. He paid dearly for stepping on her toes."

Farren seemed to realize the double meaning in her remark and immediately fell silent, but the exchange apparently broke the ice that had formed around her attitude. After grimacing a silent apology, she seemed to relax.

Conversation stopped when the waitress approached, depositing two mugs of coffee and a small pitcher of milk on the table. When she'd gone after the usual, "Anything else I can get for you ladies?" Edna said, "What made Rosie seek employment at the greenhouse?"

Farren shrugged and her smile seemed slightly malicious. "Don't know. Maybe she found out her mama wasn't quite as knowledgeable as she thought and wanted to learn some things for herself, or maybe she wanted to annoy Lily. They didn't get along, you know."

Edna ignored the last remark and asked instead, "You say Rosie was at the nursery nearly two years before her husband died?"

Farren tilted her head and frowned at the ceiling as if in thought. "Let's see, I finished their yard in the fall. That'd be a little over four years ago now." She dropped her gaze again. "Rosie applied for work late the following spring when we take on seasonal workers for the summer."

As Edna mentally calculated that Rosie must have been employed for a year before Farren's affair with Gregory Haverstrum began, his former mistress continued to explain. "I told the owners, they shouldn't hire her. I knew she wasn't serious about working, not with a rich husband and a young daughter at home, but Rosie's mother was president of Greenthumbs that year. Mel and Inez--they're the owners--they figured Lily Beck would bring in business, so they didn't listen to me. Not only that, but even after I warned them about hiring her, they assigned Rosie to my team." Farren gave a short laugh, devoid of humor. "All she did was bring scandal to the place when the news reports speculated on whether or not she murdered her husband. Of course, she quit as soon as word got out about her possible guilt. Showed Mel and Inez I was right after all."

Ignoring the pettiness of Farren's comment and the fact she seemed to forget the part she herself had played in the affair, Edna said, "Was Rosie also a designer?"

"Are you kidding?" Farren scoffed. "She didn't have the skills or the experience, regardless of her mother's reputation. I was the boss. She and the others did the grunt work. I did the thinking."

"Did she work on many projects with you?" Edna bit her tongue to keep her expression neutral, although she was beginning to dislike this self-centered, arrogant woman.

Farren looked at Edna suspiciously, but didn't hesitate with her answer. "Yes, as a matter of fact. Why do you ask?"

Edna shrugged in imitation of Farren herself. "Just wondering. The news at the time described the two of you as close friends."

Farren had the decency to look slightly embarrassed. "Being friends with an influential society dame didn't hurt me any."

Taken aback by the woman's bluntness, Edna asked something she might not have, if she had liked the woman more. "At the time, did Rosie know you were having an affair with her husband?"

To Edna's surprise, Farren didn't seem to mind the question. On the contrary, she looked almost pleased with herself. "Nah. She wasn't smart enough to notice. Frankly, I'm not sure she would have cared if she had."

"Why do you say that?"

Farren twisted her mouth into a one-sided grin. "I knew from Rosie that they'd been fighting for months."

"So the love had gone out of their marriage? Is that why Gregory turned to you and then to Bobbi Callahan?"

Farren reacted as if Edna had slapped her. Face reddening, she snapped, "He was asking for trouble when he started fooling around with the daughter of his biggest client. Duke Callahan would have killed him, if he'd known." This time, she didn't grimace at the implication of her words.

Edna was curious about one thing and hoped Farren would continue to defend herself. "If your affair was over, why did you visit Gregory the day he died?"

Farren paused for a minute as if trying to make sense of the question. When she replied, her voice was quieter and she seemed to have calmed down a little. "I went to pick up some personal belongings I'd left at his place. He kept avoiding me, wouldn't take my calls, so when I heard he was sick and laid up at home, I decided to drop in on him."

"And you took him something to eat?" Edna knew from the news reports that Farren had brought homemade soup to the invalid.

She shrugged. "I'd made beef stew for myself the night before. Stretching leftovers with some barley and broth isn't exactly rocket science, and I thought it would be better for him than the pizza deliveries he was probably living on. No big deal."

And I bet you figured you could tempt him back by playing Florence Nightingale, Edna thought, but did not say aloud. Instead, she decided to push the woman further. "Why do you think Gregory left you for someone like Bobbi Callahan? I don't know her, but I imagine you were more sophisticated and mature than a college sophomore." Edna widened her eyes with what she hoped was a look of innocence, but as long as she was baiting the woman for a reaction, she'd keep going. "Did you and he quarrel?"

Color flared in Farren's face again. "Get one thing straight, lady. He didn't leave me. I dumped him *weeks* before he picked up with his Bobbi doll. She wasn't even old enough to buy booze in this state." Farren grabbed up the shoulder bag she'd set on the seat beside her. "At any rate, it was of no concern. I'd already moved on." She stood abruptly, glancing at Edna, then down at her watch. "I have a meeting." With that, she spun on her heel and strode out of the restaurant, leaving Edna to pay the bill.

Minutes later, Edna was backing out of her parking spot when she stopped for a car that was pulling in off the street. Since the lot was narrow, being merely a strip between road and restaurant, the driver stopped, apparently waiting for Edna's spot. Dutifully, she backed out until her car was facing his. As she glanced at the man behind the wheel, recognition struck her at the same time as his face darkened. John Forrester scowled at her before fixing his eyes on the car that was driving away. Farren's bright red BMW roadster. While his attention was diverted, Edna drove over the low curb and onto the road. As she accelerated past Forrester's black Lincoln, keeping her eyes straight ahead, her heart thudded in her chest.

What is he doing here? Was he looking for Farren? Has he been following me? Reconsidering the last thought, Edna scolded herself. *Stop being paranoid. He's probably here for lunch.* At that moment, the thought struck her ... even if it were purely coincidental that he had shown up at the Harborside Café, it wouldn't take a genius to figure out that Edna had been talking to Farren.

Chapter 15

Edna decided not to go home, at least not yet. John Forrester knew where she lived and she didn't want to chance an encounter with him, if he took it into his head to pay her another unannounced visit. She drove to one of the largest of the local malls and parked in the middle of a row where her car might blend in with others in the lot. She'd kept an eye on her rear view mirror and was fairly certain Forrester hadn't followed her, but she knew from watching her favorite TV detective shows that expert investigators could be crafty when it came to trailing someone.

He might be watching her right now, but she couldn't very well sit in her car all day, nor did she wish to walk around the stores simply to kill time. Should she go see how Tuck and Peppa were getting along? Maybe she'd better organize her thoughts before she did anything else.

Rummaging in her tote bag, she took out a small notebook and pencil and began to jot down the questions she had surrounding Peppa's problem.

How did Clem end up at the foot of Peppa's driveway? According to Charlie, both Clem's truck and Lily's Impala were in the garage, so he hadn't driven. Someone had cleared the snow off the driveway, so it was impossible to tell if or when the cars had last been moved.

Had he walked? Edna thought it was fairly certain Clem wouldn't have trudged three miles on a stormy night before collapsing less than a hundred yards from Peppa's doorstep, but she wrote down the question anyway.

Was he already dead when Peppa drove over him? That was the tough question and one the medical examiner would have to answer.

If Peppa's Mercedes hadn't killed him, had he died of natural causes? Again, the answer would have to wait for the medical examiner's report.

Why was he clutching a Christmas Rose? Noting *Lily Beck* in the margin, Edna wondered with an inward groan how she would approach that question.

So deep in thought was she that the sudden appearance of two women getting into the car to her left startled her. Not two minutes later, the owner of the pickup, parked on her right, got in and drove away. Sitting in her car with two empty slots on one side and one on the other, she felt exposed. Looking around cautiously, she started the car and moved to the next row, pulling in between an SUV and a van with the name of a plumbing company on the side. Feeling somewhat easier now and more than a little silly, she picked up the notebook and pencil again. Leaving a few blank pages, she began noting questions she had about the Haverstrum death.

Gossip at the time was that there were symptoms included in the autopsy report that may or may not have been related to his heart failure. She would ask Charlie what he knew about that. *Could Lily have administered some of her 'special medicine' that Lettie spoke of? Had Lily thought to cure her son-in-law and ended up killing him instead?* Edna thought of her own recent education on the unpredictability of the strength of plants grown in one's garden. Those used for medicinal purposes could just as well cause an overdose, if a season's soil and weather conditions created more potent vegetation. She decided to find out from Lily if she were interested in herbal medicine. Did she actually use what she concocted to treat illness, or was that simply something she said to Lettie to satisfy a child's curiosity? Again, Edna might have to tread carefully on that point.

Why was John Forrester investigating the case? Another thing she'd ask Charlie. He might know or be able to find out, she thought, marking his initials in the margin. She remembered in some of the novels she'd read and shows she'd watched that some retired cops, finding time on their hands, looked into old crimes. Was that what Forrester was doing? It certainly seemed that he thought a crime had been committed, despite any evidence to prove it, so Edna approached her next questions with that in mind.

Who benefited from Gregory Haverstrum's death? She thought Rosie was probably the main beneficiary, but she'd check to be certain. Edna remembered Rosie saying she never received his life insurance, but it was unlikely that insurance would have been his only asset. If a significant inheritance had been at stake, certainly the papers would have been full of it, but no reports had mentioned Haverstrum's finances. Had he even written a will? If not, all his worldly goods would automatically have gone to his wife, Edna thought. The Haverstrums had lived in an expensive house, but they could have been up to their eyeballs in debt.

A picture of Lily Beck's home popped into Edna's mind. It was neat and clean, but decidedly shabby. And her clothes had obviously been expensive, but they were dated and threadbare as well. Apparently, Lily had to watch her budget. Edna thought of the obvious tension between Rosie and her mother. *If Rosie had money, wouldn't she help her mother maintain the family home or buy her a new outfit?* Edna supposed Rosie would probably not be employed as an assistant to an event planner if she didn't have to work.

What else might have motivated someone to murder Gregory Haverstrum? Edna didn't think Rosie would kill her husband simply because he'd been cheating on her. Maybe the motive wasn't money or sex, but something else like revenge. If not his wife, could an angry business associate have wanted Haverstrum dead? Maybe she should check on whether or not any of his clients had lost a considerable amount of money because of his advice.

Edna's head began to throb. Too many questions and not nearly enough answers. Going back over the pages, she realized that one person was definitely associated with both deaths. Obviously, her next step was to speak with Lily Beck. Edna thought again of the ex-detective who also was connected to both cases. Why had Forrester shown up at the scene of Clem's death? The handyman could hardly have had anything to do with what had happened to Gregory Haverstrum. Clem hadn't even been living in the area two years ago.

As Edna was about to start her car, she had a

dreadful thought. What if Forrester were to see her at Lily's? She felt her temper rise at the bullying attitude of that man. He had no authority to tell her what she could or couldn't do, and she knew part of her anger was at herself for allowing him to intimidate her. She could very well be on garden club business or even offering condolences over Clem. The retired policeman could assume Edna was asking about the deaths of the handyman or the son-in-law, but he couldn't prove a thing.

Now, all she had to do was think of an excuse to give Lily for dropping by unannounced. A sympathy visit over the loss of her worker was weak, but it would have to do. *I'll take her some flowers*, Edna thought, then immediately laughed at herself. *What's the expression? Taking coals to Newcastle?* She thought then of the sketch she'd done, meaning for it to be a thank-you for last month's invitation to view Lily's winter garden. Under the circumstances, Edna knew she'd never be able to give that particular present to Lily, ever. A drawing of the Christmas Rose would be a terrible and gruesome reminder. Edna considered keeping it for herself, but immediately rejected the idea. She couldn't help but think of Clem lying in the snow when she saw the blossom. Not only that, but if she were to hang the painting in her house, there was always a chance that Peppa or Tuck would spot it. She decided to burn it in the fireplace as soon as she got home.

After a moment's thought and scanning the storefronts that weren't blocked by the SUV to her left, Edna decided to visit a small tea shop where she bought a tin of her favorite English Breakfast tea and a box of fancy chocolate digestives. The boutique's small paper bag with string handles was attractive enough to serve as gift wrapping.

Hoping Lily would be pleased with the gift and anxious to talk about recent events, Edna headed for the Beck house. As she drove, she began to wonder about Lily's family. Why had Rosie taken Lettie home after the youngster had been with her grandmother for only a day? Supposedly, the girl was to stay the week because Rosie had to work long hours preparing for several Valentine's Day weddings. Was it Rosie who needed to have Lettie near her or was the little girl afraid her mother would go away just as her father had done?

Pulling onto the broad driveway, Edna spotted Lily bent over in the garden, seeming to tamp down dirt with the blade of a small shovel. The woman straightened as Edna turned off the engine. Neither Lily's nor Clem's vehicle was in sight. Getting out of the car, Edna glanced at the windows of the apartment above the garage and idly wondered who would clear out Clem's belongings or if he'd even had very much to begin with. She speculated if anything in his place might provide a clue to what had happened to him. She might offer her help to pack up his things and take them to Peppa.

These thoughts were interrupted as Lily waved her over. When Edna approached, she could see Lily looked disgusted.

"That wretched man uprooted my Christmas Rose."

Edna looked at the tangle of roots, leaves and a few mangled blossoms. "I assume you mean Clem. Did you see him do it?"

Lily frowned as if the thought hadn't occurred to

her. "Well, no. I didn't actually *see* him do it. I would have stopped him if I had. That female police officer was here not an hour ago. Showed me a picture on her phone and asked if I recognized it. Well, of course, I came straight out here and found this." Lily flapped her hand at the churned-up soil.

"Maybe someone else did the damage and he only picked up one of the blooms."

Lily turned on her, sounding half angry and half curious. "Who would do such a thing?"

"I have no idea. I'm just wondering why Clem would destroy your plant and attempt to take a bloom to his ex-wife, particularly since he hadn't seen her in years."

Lily poked her shovel around in the dirt. "I don't know who else would have done such a thing. Certainly not my daughter or my granddaughter. They wouldn't dare. And you've just confirmed my suspicion. If Clem didn't do this, why would he be carrying around one of the blooms?"

Edna shook her head. "Wish I knew."

As if the thought had just occurred to her, Lily eyed Edna inquisitively. "I don't often see you in this neighborhood."

Edna suddenly felt awkward. She should have realized from the way she'd seen Lily treat Clem on Friday that the woman had little feeling for the man who'd worked for her these last several months. Edna plowed on, still hoping to gain something from the visit. "I thought you might be upset over your handyman's death." She held up the bag from the tea shop. "I came to offer my sympathy and bring condolences," thinking again as she spoke the words that the woman didn't appear to need comforting.

Lily seemed to soften considerably, but not, Edna suspected, over the memory of her employee. Maybe she wasn't used to receiving gifts from acquaintances. "How nice of you," she said, her face flushing with pleasure. Pushing the shovel into the loose soil next to the demolished Christmas Rose, she reached for the present and peeked inside. "Lovely." She looked up at Edna and smiled. "Let's go inside and I'll brew a pot."

Exactly what Edna had hoped and she was suddenly glad she'd thought to bring that particular gift. With Clem being foremost in her mind, when she followed Lily into the kitchen, Edna said, "I didn't know when I met him the other day that your handyman was the ex-husband of my friend Harriet Peppafitch."

"And I didn't realize you were acquainted with Peppa," Lily said. "I used to take Rose to Saturday story hour at the library."

Edna couldn't tell by Lily's bland expression what she thought of Peppa, so decided to continue with the excuse for her visit. "I thought if I could tell Peppa about Clem's work here and particularly his last days, she might find some solace." *Who knows*, Edna thought, *that tiny white lie may turn out to be the truth.* Aloud, she said, "Can you tell me anything about him that I could take back to her? Aside from his work for you, was he involved in anything else? Hobbies, perhaps, or maybe he spent time with friends in the area? Maybe he reconnected with some of his old colleagues?"

"Let me think," Lily said, having filled an electric kettle with water and turned it on. Falling silent while she pulled the tea tin and biscuit box out of the small bag, she seemed to concentrate more on her gifts than Edna's questions. She put some digestives on a plate and reached for a white porcelain teapot decorated with violets. Disappearing into the dining room, she returned with two china cups and saucers which she set on a wooden tray alongside the biscuits.

By the time Lily had finished setting things out, the water was boiling, so she poured some into the pot. When the porcelain was warm enough for her apparent satisfaction, she poured out the water, spooned tea leaves into the pot and carefully refilled it. That done, she covered it with a cozy and turned to Edna with a smile. "If you'll carry the tray, we'll go sit in the conservatory. It's my favorite room, especially on a sunny winter day like today."

Admiring Lily's proper way to make a pot of tea, Edna followed her hostess to the bright, glassed-in room at the back of the house. When they were settled in cushioned wicker chairs, she posed a different question. "How did Clem come to work for you? You said you knew Peppa from the library, but had you known her husband? I understand they separated about five years ago and he left town."

Lily, slowly turning the pot three rotations to settle the tea leaves, didn't answer immediately. When she finally did, it was with a nod. "Yes, I knew him as Professor Peppafitch. I took a class from him … oh, let's see, about fifteen years ago, maybe twenty. I forget exactly which one he taught. I audited several at the university about the same time." She poured out a cup for Edna and handed it to her. "He must have

remembered that I keep to myself and never gossip."
She sat back in her chair, carefully balancing her cup
and saucer. "I think that's why he knocked on my door
when he came back to town. Knew I wouldn't spread his
business around."

"Did he ever mention to you why he didn't want his
ex-wife to know he was back?"

Lily shook her head. "Nope. Didn't ask and he
didn't offer. I keep myself to myself, and he did, too."
She looked at Edna as if the question were slightly
offensive. "Besides, we weren't exactly social equals.
He worked for me."

Edna ignored the snobbish remark and asked. "Was
he in touch with any of his old friends? Did anyone
come to visit?"

"Not that I knew of. Never saw anyone talking to
him. Nobody ever came to my door looking for him."

Edna thought she'd probably exhausted this line of
inquiry, so she sipped her tea as she considered how to
get Lily to talk about her late son-in-law. Hoping there
was a soft spot somewhere in the woman, Edna said,
"My granddaughter told me that Lettie … I mean Violet,
went home with her mother." When Lily simply stared
out the glass walls at the garden beyond, Edna went on.
"I thought from what Amanda said that Violet would be
staying with you for the entire week. I was looking
forward to saying hello to her again. She's a delightful
child and I enjoyed her company on Saturday." Edna
thought that was laying it on pretty thick, but she hoped
her effusiveness would encourage Lily to talk about her
family.

"Her mother changed our plans." Edna noticed a

faint flush creeping up the woman's neck to her cheek and thought she heard a muttered "typical" before Lily's lips tightened into a firm line. She surprised Edna by speaking again. "She's too fiercely protective of the child. Girl's not able to breath the way Rose hovers."

Sensing a tense frustration to that bit of conversation, Edna tried again, hoping to lighten Lily's mood. "Rosie … ah, Rose says Violet is happier since they moved to Warwick. Do you get that impression also?"

This time, Lily did turn her head and her lips loosened into a near smile. "Yes, I do think she seems more cheerful lately."

Without thinking, Edna spoke from her heart. "I believe that if the rumors surrounding her father's death were put to rest, Lettie could be saved from future persecution."

Lily stood abruptly and dropped her cup and saucer on the table, nearly shattering the fine bone china. "If you don't mind, Edna, I will get back to my garden."

Chapter 16

Edna had known the son-in-law's death and subsequent effects on his family would be a difficult subject to broach, but it had been worth a try. Or had it? Would Lily ever speak to her again? And what had made her so angry? Was it the possibility of Lettie being the brunt of other children's brutality that upset Lily or was it mention of Gregory Haverstrum? How close had she been to her daughter's husband?

Edna sighed. She'd driven away without much thought to where she was going, but as if by instinct, she was heading toward her own neighborhood. Glancing at the dashboard clock, she saw it was nearly noon. Seeing no other traffic on the straightaway, she pulled onto the shoulder and took out her cell phone to call Charlie.

"Have you had lunch?" she asked after greeting the detective and finding out he was at his desk in the stationhouse.

"Are you offering or wanting me to take you out?" he replied with a smile in his voice.

She laughed. "I'm not quite certain what's in the larder, but if you want to take a chance, I'm offering."

"I'll take a chance on your cooking any day. Shall I drop around in a half hour?"

"That will be fine." Ending the call and pulling back onto the road, she began mentally to line up the questions she had for him. And, if John Forrester did show up unannounced, he would be in for a surprise. Edna grinned at the thought, almost wishing the retired policeman would arrive on her doorstep while Charlie was there.

Forty minutes later, she heard a knock at the back door and a voice call from the mud room. "Hi, Edna. It's me."

"Come in, Charlie," she called back from the stove where she was stirring bits of ham into a pot of split-pea soup. He'd removed his coat and was walking into the kitchen when a dinging noise sounded. "Perfect timing," she said and pulled a pan of corn bread out of the oven. "Pour yourself a cup of coffee and sit."

Over lunch, they chatted about things unrelated to any police investigation, except for Charlie to bemoan the fact that work had interfered with a special dinner date with Starling. When her name came up, Edna was careful to stay away from asking questions of a too-personal nature. She wondered if she appeared too eager or pushy, if she would scare Charlie away from her daughter. The two young people would find their way together or not, but Edna had to admit she was getting impatient for them to realize they were meant for each other.

When they reached a dessert of cranberry cake, Edna refilled Charlie's coffee, served herself a cup of tea and started in on her reason for inviting the detective to lunch. "Have you gotten a report from the medical examiner about Clem?"

"Not yet, but something else has surfaced. I told him about the ranunculin you mentioned as possibly causing the mouth ulcers. He said Clem's mouth and esophagus were clean, but the blisters you mentioned rang a bell in an older case."

"A poisoning?"

Charlie nodded. "Yup. Gregory Haverstrum. He had those exact symptoms. At the time, the M.E. didn't know for sure the blisters were related to cause of death, but he found nothing he could test for. Without an idea of what he'd be looking for, it'd be a waste of taxpayers' money to go off on a fishing expedition. So, the investigating team noted the abnormality in Haverstrum's file, but didn't think much more about it. They figured it probably was related to the flu that had him laid up that week."

Edna felt her pulse speed up. "Can the M.E. recheck a two-year-old corpse?"

"Afraid not. Haverstrum was cremated as soon as his body was released."

Edna sank back in her chair, having realized her mistake. "Ranunculin's a natural substance. It's likely it had dissipated anyway before Gregory's body was found. Two days, wasn't it?"

Charlie nodded, paused, then said, "Well, the M.E. has the information now, so I trust he'll know what to do with it if he ever spots those symptoms again. At any rate, Clem didn't have skin lesions, so we struck out there."

"How did he happen to collapse in Peppa's driveway, and how did he get there in the first place?"

"Seems he was on foot, at least part of the way. Neighbor stepped outside about nine o'clock to walk her dog. Thought our description of Clem sounded like a man she saw stumbling down the street. She lives at the opposite end of the block from Peppa's house. Said the man was a couple of houses away with his back to her, so she only got an impression. She figured he was a drunk, stumbling home. Didn't think much more about it until we knocked on her door when we canvased the neighborhood."

"Surely Clem couldn't have walked all the way from Lily Beck's to Peppa's, particularly if he were drunk," Edna said. "That must be … what … at least three miles."

Charlie shook his head, more in bewilderment than denial. "You're right. Can't think he could have made it that far under his own steam, but his truck was in the garage. Lily's car, too. Someone must have given him a ride. We're thinking maybe he hitched and got dropped off somewhere nearby. That could explain it. Reporters are getting the story out, asking for anyone who might have picked him up to contact us. It's a long shot, but it's all we got right now."

"I suppose you questioned Lily about her comings and goings Saturday night. The way she treated him when I was there, I can't imagine she'd offer to drive him anywhere." Edna thought of something else. "According to her daughter, Lily doesn't drive if the weather is bad or even if it *looks* like it will be bad."

Charlie nodded. "She was one of the first people we interviewed. Said she hadn't left the house. She said her daughter and granddaughter were with her the entire evening. They had dinner together, then decided to watch a movie on TV. Lily said partway through the show, she began to feel queasy and went to bed after taking an antacid. Left Rose and Violet around seven and didn't see them again until Rose came into her room at five thirty Sunday morning."

"Five thirty?" Edna asked, surprised at the news. "Why so early?"

"Apparently, Rose had to go to work. Told her mother that she promised her boss to make up for not working late Saturday afternoon."

"And she took Violet back to Warwick with her," Edna interjected.

"That's right. Lily said she dozed off again for an hour and when she got up, she realized her granddaughter was gone. Called Rose just to make certain the girl was with her. Seemed angry that her daughter hadn't mentioned it when she left."

Edna thought for a minute while she sipped tea. She couldn't think of anything else to ask Charlie about Clem until the M.E.'s report was in. She wasn't finished picking his brain, though. "Besides the blistering and the fact that Gregory was cremated, what else do you know about the investigation?"

"The Haverstrum case?" Charlie held his mug out when Edna lifted the coffee pot in a silent offer of a refill, then settled back in his chair. "From what I remember, he was found by his cleaning woman. As you already know, he'd been dead about two days. He was home with the flu before that, so nobody missed him. No broken appointments or things of that sort that would have sent someone around sooner. There were rumors about food poisoning, others about possible suicide. The body was in pretty bad shape. He'd been pretty sick before he died. Also, the heat in his condo had been turned up. Granted, it was wintertime, but the temperature was near ninety in his place. A dead body in those conditions deteriorates faster than normal." Charlie sat forward to set his coffee cup on the table. "Reporters had a number of theories, probably to sell papers, but nothing amounted to much as far as the investigating team was concerned. Most of what they found in his place was chalked up to his illness."

Edna was confused. "If everything was ruled out, why is John Forrester trying to pin something on Rosie?"

"Are you sure that's what he's doing?" Before she could respond, Charlie went on. "From what I know, she went to the condo and cleaned up. Several people had brought casseroles or soups to Haverstrum. You know, the sort of thing folks do for sick friends who are helpless around the house." Charlie grinned at Edna as if he were speaking from personal experience.

She smiled in return, but absently. She was thinking of Rosie's visit to her estranged husband's abode. "I assume the timing worked out to prove Gregory was still alive when she left him?"

"So she claimed in her statement. She said she'd stopped in to see if he needed anything. Everyone else was bringing him food, so she was only checking on him. Said she knew he had a cleaning woman, but the kitchen was such a mess, she figured she'd straighten it up."

"She was being pretty nice to him, considering how badly he'd treated her."

Charlie shook his head. "I'll never understand it, but some marriages are like that. Wife can't live with her husband, but can't seem to live without him, either."

"And vice versa," Edna added.

"And vice versa," Charlie agreed.

"Let me guess," Edna said, returning to the subject. "Detective Forrester doesn't buy it that Rosie cleaned up when she knew Gregory had a cleaning woman coming in."

Charlie raised his eyebrows. "You're onto this detective business pretty well, Mrs. Davies."

Edna felt a glow of pleasure over the compliment, but was also a little surprised. "I thought I was being sarcastic. Does he really think like that? After all, the housekeeper wasn't expected for a couple more days. Right? If the kitchen were dirty, her washing up would make sense to me."

Charlie nodded. "To give John his due, Rosie's efforts were confined to the kitchen. She said Gregory had taken food out of the refrigerator, left stuff in pots on the stove, took lids off dishes to see what was inside and hadn't put anything back. According to her, some things were beginning to mold and some to smell up the place, so she ground the garbage in the disposal and ran the pots and pans through the dishwasher. At the time, our investigators suspected she did that to destroy evidence." Charlie shrugged as if to say, *her motive is anyone's guess.*

"But," Edna speculated, "because the medical examiner didn't find anything unusual in Gregory's body, nobody could prove foul play."

"That's right."

"And you don't think John Forrester is trying to implicate Rosie in the death of her husband?"

Charlie shrugged again. "Seems like you're jumping to conclusions just because he's asking questions about an old case. Maybe he's curious."

"But why that particular case? Didn't you say he'd been taken off it, less than a day after the body was found?"

"Right again." Charlie turned his wrist to look at his watch. "Uh, oh. I gotta get back to work." He rose and bent to give Edna a quick peck on the cheek. "Thanks for lunch."

After he'd gone, Edna thought about her last question. *Why indeed was John Forrester investigating a case he was never really on in the first place?*

Chapter 17

"You home, Edna?"

Mary's voice reached Edna about the same time that Hank rested his muzzle on her lap, tail happily wagging. Ink Spot jumped onto the chair beside the one on which Benjamin sat looking much like a miniature Sphinx. The black cat then stepped delicately across to the ginger cat's cushion before sitting on an edge, nonchalantly beginning to lick a paw.

Once the lunch dishes had been cleared and the kitchen cleaned, Edna had spent the afternoon running a few errands before returning home to a cup of tea and her thoughts. Her mind had been racing and the tea cooling as Mary let herself and her companions in through the mudroom.

"Hi, neighbor." Glad for the distraction, Edna lifted the cozy and felt the tea pot to find it had grown as cold as the liquid in her cup. "I could use a warmer. How about you?"

"Wouldn't mind." Mary placed a large book on the table next to Edna's elbow before sitting opposite and resting her forearms on the table. The book's cover was a faded brown with "A History of Rhode Island, Colonial Days to the Great War" in faded gold lettering.

"What's this?" Edna picked up the old book and scanned the title page and table of contents. The tome was at least two inches thick and heavy, its pages yellowed with age.

"It was in our library," Mary said. "Belonged to my grandfather. He collected books, mostly history. I've been doin' research."

"On your ghost. So Starling told me. You look more rested today. Has he gone?"

"No. He's still running around up there. I just got up from a nap. Came over to give you my new theory. Get your opinion."

Setting the book aside, Edna rose to fill the kettle and place it on the stove while Hank moved to settle on the floor next to the cats' chair. As she returned to the table for the porcelain pot, she raised her eyebrows. "A new theory?"

Mary nodded. "I've been readin' this book to find out what I can about the area. Figured it might give me a clue to my ghost. You know, who he is and why he's suddenly become restless. Found a chapter on early slavery in Rhode Island. Our house was a station on the Underground Railroad." She announced the latter with some pride.

"Really?" Edna was intrigued.

"Yup," Mary's head bobbed and an amused grin spread across her face. "One time, when Nanny wasn't lookin', I snuck into the storage side of the attic. I wasn't allowed in that room, so of course that's where I wanted to explore. I discovered a hiding place in the chimney."

"Oh?" Edna said, smiling at her mental image of a child as unmanageable as her carroty-red, curly hair. Fascinated by the Osbourne mansion's past, Edna listened intently as she poured hot water into the pot to warm it and reached for the tin of loose tea.

"There's a false front on two sides of the big chimney in the storage area, above Father's old rooms."

Edna thought of her night in the bedroom over the kitchen after Tom Greene had been killed. She'd stayed with Mary when the Davieses' house had been broken into and Edna's life had been threatened. She remembered with some guilt, sneaking down the back stairs in an attempt to escape from Mary who, Edna suspected at the time, had dangerous intentions.

"It's where the runaway slaves hid when bounty hunters came looking for them." Mary's voice broke into Edna's reflections, as her story continued. "Father discovered I'd found the secret place, and he told me that when that addition was built onto the main house shortly before the Civil War, the masons added the extra brick to the chimney. He said there was also supposed to be a secret passage in the house, but he didn't know where. He thought it must be between the new section and the original outside wall, maybe a secret stairway up to the attic or down to the dirt cellar. Off and on, growing up, I used to try to find it." Mary chucked. "I probably drove poor Nanny crazy, knocking on the walls, trying to figure out if they were hollow. Forgot all about it 'til I started readin' about the abolitionists."

"That's interesting," Edna said, bringing the freshly brewed tea to the table. "I'd like to see the old chimney hideout sometime."

Mary nodded and went on with her narrative, leaving Edna relieved her neighbor hadn't used the impulsive remark to begin pressuring Edna to spend the night. Instead, Mary pulled the book closer to her and rested a hand on the cover. "Did you know Rhode Island was the first of the original thirteen colonies to ban slavery?"

Edna shook her head, reseating herself at the table. "No, I didn't."

Mary's brow creased in puzzlement. "That part of the history confuses me 'cause it also says Rhode Island had twice as many slaves as any other colony. After the Revolutionary War, Rhode Island merchants controlled more than half the trade in African slaves. That was part of the Triangle Trade I remember learning about in school. You know, when molasses was shipped to New England to make rum, and then the rum was shipped to Africa to trade for slaves who were transported to the sugar plantations in the Caribbean so more molasses could be produced. And around and around it went," she said, rolling her head as if to demonstrate the unending circle.

Edna was interested, but bewildered. "I think we've gotten off the subject. What does all that old history have to do with your ghost? Do you suspect he's hiding in the chimney?"

Mary shook her head vigorously. "No, no. Not necessarily. Don't you see? The chimney only proves that people hid up there. The ghost might be an escaped slave who died in the attic, but he could just as well have been killed in the nearby woods and his spirit made it to the house because it was a safe place."

"Don't you think you're going a bit overboard with these ghost theories of yours? Maybe you should call an exterminator and have them look for whatever wild animal is hiding under the eaves."

Mary looked crestfallen. "You haven't heard those sounds. It isn't a wild animal. If you'd come spend a night, you'd know what I'm talking about."

Not quite ready to go ghost-busting, Edna knew a sure-fire way to distract Mary was police business. Noncommittally, she said, "Okay. I will, but not tonight. Right now, Amanda's friend Lettie is on my mind. You might be able to help me try to figure something out."

Mary's eyes brightened as she picked up her tea mug and held it between her hands. Before taking a sip, she said, "Sure. What is it?"

"What do you know about the scandal surrounding Gregory Haverstrum's death?"

The redhead frowned in bewilderment. "That was a coupla years ago. Why do you want to know about that?"

"Remember when I was suspected of poisoning Tom?"

Mary nodded, but didn't speak.

"Well, Rosie Beck is living under the same dark cloud as I was before Tom's murderer was caught. Thank goodness the investigation didn't drag out and affect my family, but unfortunately that's not the case with Rosie, and I learned recently that Gregory's daughter Lettie is being taunted by her classmates. Right now, Amanda is her only friend. I'm very worried that sooner or later my granddaughter's friends will turn on her, too … or, if not their classmates, the parents will forbid their children to associate with the girls."

Mary slouched in her chair, her mouth twisting in a smile that held no humor. "Kids can be cruel," she said, and Edna suspected her neighbor was speaking from personal experience.

Was it the carroty-red, unmanageable hair that her playmates ridiculed or Mary's lanky height or maybe the fact that she had a nanny? Anything that made a child stand out from the rest was fodder for juvenile mockery, Edna thought with a mental shake of her head. Aloud, she said, "I'd like to help that poor girl by finding out what exactly happened to her father. I don't expect to uncover any new facts, but maybe I can provide a different perspective and something will pop out that nobody considered significant at the time. Selfishly, I don't want the injustice to smear anyone in my son's family, either."

Mary straightened and looked determined. "I'll tell you what I can. Why don't you tell me what you already know? That'll help jog my memory."

Edna agreed and looked up at the wall clock. "It's nearly five. Near enough that I suggest we switch from tea to wine and go sit in the living room. It's warmed up enough to melt the latest snowfall, but the house feels cold. I think a small fire in the hearth would feel good, don't you?"

In full agreement, Mary opened a bottle of merlot while Edna arranged a plate of cheese and crackers. Carrying everything to a more comfortable setting, Edna turned on a couple of table lamps while Mary built a small fire to take the late-afternoon chill from the room. Finally, sitting back in her favorite chair, across the coffee table from where Mary sat on the sofa, Edna began to relay what she'd learned from the Internet and from the people with whom she'd spoken, so far.

"Gregory had been housebound with the flu in the days leading up to his death. Several people stopped in to visit during that time, and a few brought him food. Apparently, the man didn't cook for himself, even when he was healthy, but he did seem able to warm things up." Edna paused to take a sip of wine as she made a mental list of Haverstrum's callers. "Rosie came by twice that week. That seemed strange to me, since their recent separation had not been amicable."

"Maybe Rosie went to see him because of Lettie," Mary suggested. "Did the girl visit her father ?"

"Once, I believe, with her grandmother, apparently against Rosie's wishes," Edna said. "That's what made me wonder about Rosie. She hadn't wanted her daughter to catch whatever was ailing Gregory, but she could have carried it back and given it to Lettie herself." Edna was thoughtful for a few seconds before continuing, "Lily accompanied her granddaughter on a first visit and then made a second visit herself the morning before Gregory died." Almost absently, Edna added, "I wonder how she got along with her son-in-law."

Mary shrugged as if the answer didn't matter. "Who else went to see him?" she asked before taking a sip from her glass and settling more comfortably into the corner of the couch.

"Let's see," said Edna, recalling the news stories. "Farren McCree, whom the reporters referred to as his old mistress. I wonder if they meant 'former' or were mocking her because she was quite a few years older than Gregory. Her showing up also surprised me, since rumor was that he'd dumped her to take up with his new office assistant Bobbi Callahan." At the mention of

Farren, Edna remembered what the woman had said and passed it along to Mary. "According to Farren, she was the one who broke off the affair."

"She might say that to save face," Mary opined. "I bet it was Gregory who did the breaking up 'cause Bobbi's father was one of Haverstrum's biggest clients. Duke Callahan got her the job. She was a college sophomore, studying business before she switched her major to education. Mr. Callahan thought practical experience would do her some good. Wonder how he felt when he learned his friend took advantage of the daughter. I seem to remember reporters referred to her as 'Bobbi Doll'. Can't imagine he'd been pleased about that, either."

Edna waited to see if Mary would add any more information. When she didn't, Edna said, "Young Miss Callahan dropped by to see Gregory, of course. Besides some sort of soup she'd bought at a deli, she had contracts for him to look over and checks to sign."

"Anyone else show up?" Mary asked. She was stroking Ink Spot who had jumped into her lap. Benjamin was in his bed by the hearth, and Hank had stretched out on the area rug next to the sofa.

Edna recounted, "Rosie, Lily, Farren, Bobbi … oh, yes, and Duke Callahan himself. He was mentioned in the reports because he didn't come forward until police talked to a neighbor who said she'd seen him going into the condo the evening Gregory was thought to have died. Callahan claimed he went to the door, but when Gregory didn't answer his knock, he left without entering the place. Said he neither saw nor spoke to Gregory that night."

"That's right," Mary said, sitting up to put her wine glass on the coffee table. She then melted back into the corner of the couch as she recalled. "I remember now … I heard he was summoned to the police station after a patrol officer discovered he'd been there. Mr. Callahan wasn't very popular, particularly when he showed up with a lawyer, but I think he's good friends with the chief so no rumors came out in the papers."

Mention of the police and the investigation prompted Edna to ask, "Do you know John Forrester?"

"Don't know him personally, but I've heard some talk." Mary's grimace told Edna some of what she wanted to know.

"What have you heard?"

"That he grovels before anyone he thinks has power and bullies everyone else. He's arrogant and a sexist. When he was still on the force, he acted oh-so-nice when other detectives or officers were within earshot, but he could be mean as a coiled snake, mostly to the women. Treated them like something to scrape off his shoe. They all hated him."

"How did he get away with it? He must have been reprimanded for his behavior."

Mary leaned forward to select a cracker and a slice of cheese before settling back and answering Edna. "I guess nobody ever had enough proof to bring an official complaint. He probably made sure of that." She paused and studied the food in her hand for a few seconds. "Come to think of it, there was some gossip last year that retirement wasn't his idea. Some believe he was asked to leave."

The thought suddenly struck Edna that Forrester

might have left the force in order to pursue the old investigation. "Do you know anything about his being taken off the case the day after Haverstrum's body was found?"

Mary frowned. "Nope. That raised some eyebrows at the time, but nothing ever leaked about what went on between the chief and his newest detective. Forrester was out of town for a couple of weeks. 'Training,' so it was said."

"What else do you know about him? Is he married? Did he grow up around here?"

Mary shook her head. "Don't know much before he got to town. Moved here from a small town in western Massachusetts, near the New York border, I think. He heard about a job on the force here, applied and got it. I think a former chief of his recommended him for the position. Somethin' like that."

"How long ago was that?"

Mary squinted up at the ceiling for a few seconds before answering. "Must be about four years now."

"Not that long ago," Edna muttered, more to herself than to Mary. "Why did he leave his last job to come here? If he wanted to advance in law enforcement, you'd think he'd apply to a big city department, wouldn't you?"

Mary frowned and hesitated a few seconds before admitting, "Don't know."

Edna thought again of Forrester's unexpected visit to her doorstep. "Do you think he's dangerous? Do you know if he's ever been violent?"

"Coupla times, he was suspected of roughing up guys who tried to resist arrest--or who he *claimed* resisted, but nobody ever pressed charges."

It wasn't exactly the answer Edna wanted to hear. Dropping Forrester for the time being, she was about to ask Mary what else she remembered about Gregory Haverstrum when Hank stood up suddenly and poked his muzzle into Mary's side. It must have tickled because the redhead laughed as she gently pushed the Labrador away.

"Sorry, Edna. This old fella is saying it's time for his supper. Probably time for a walk, too."

Edna was disappointed that Mary couldn't stay longer and discuss the scandal. Alone and at loose ends, she decided to phone Albert. When she was switched immediately to his voice mail, she tried Matthew's number with the same result. Determined, she pressed the speed dial for her son-in-law Roger, and when he didn't respond, she began to wonder. Since it was unusual that she couldn't raise at least one of the men, she called Irene and was relieved to hear a voice that wasn't filled with panic.

"Sorry, Edna. I was supposed to let you know they are spending the night at sea. Everyone agreed they wanted a peaceful evening with no ringing phones, so all the devices are off. First one who turns his back on has to buy the next case of beer."

Edna chuckled along with her daughter-in-law over the inevitable bets and then asked about the children.

Irene didn't answer immediately and enthusiastically, as she usually did. Instead, the silence on the other end of the line dragged on for so long that Edna began to wonder if she'd been disconnected. She was about to speak when she heard her daughter-in-law's low voice, as if she didn't want anyone else to hear. "Can you come for supper tomorrow night? The kids would love to see you, and Lettie will be here, too."

"Lettie?" Edna was puzzled, more by Irene's lowered tone than the words.

"Yes. She's been staying with us."

Edna was surprised and, although she didn't express her doubts to Irene, wondered why Rosie would remove her daughter from the grandmother's care, only to put Lettie in the hands of a relative stranger. *Most peculiar and erratic behavior*, Edna thought.

Chapter 18

When Irene told Edna that Lettie was going to hang out with Amanda for the entire day, Edna decided to drive to Warwick earlier than suppertime. She wanted to arrive well before Rosie got off work and came to the house. Edna's excuse would be that she wanted to give the girls a special day by taking them shopping and out for lunch. Afterwards, they could have an afternoon of hair styling and manicures. Irene was excited about the idea, and Edna suspected some adult company for a stay-at-home mom was part of the appeal.

Tuesday morning, on her way to Warwick, Edna wondered again why Rosie had removed her daughter from Lily's care, only to leave the child with a neighbor. Irene would be responsible for the girl this entire week, at least while Rosie was at work. Irene said she didn't mind, she had to be home with Amanda anyway, but Edna thought it presumptuous of Rosie to impose on Irene's generous nature. Edna hoped the two mothers had come to some sort of day-care agreement, but then doubted Irene would take any recompense for what she'd consider "just being neighborly." *Still*, thought Edna, and stopped there.

Knowing it was futile to speculate, her thoughts turned to the deaths of two men. As far as she knew, Gregory and Clem hadn't even known each other, but she couldn't help a nagging suspicion that their deaths were somehow connected. Gregory Haverstrum had suspicious burns around his mouth, symptomatic of the type of poison produced by the Christmas Rose. Clem Peppafitch had the same plant clutched in his hand, but no telltale blisters. Because of that one blossom, Edna sensed a link to both fatalities, but how? More importantly, why?

She thought back to Lettie's comment about her grandmother's making "medicine" from the plant. Was Lily responsible for her son-in-law's death or, if Edna was correct and the two deaths were connected, Clem's fatality? What would Lily have gained by killing either man?

Edna was giving herself a headache. Was she letting her imagination get the better of her? She needed to find out for certain how Clem died and didn't want to believe it was by Peppa's Mercedes.

Her mind segued back to images of Lily's daughter and granddaughter. Did Rosie suspect her mother of murder? Is that why she'd rather leave Lettie with neighbors than with her grandmother? Were those fears the cause of the tension between the two women?

Because of Edna's strong feelings that Clem's death was related to Gregory's, she wanted to talk with both Lettie and Rosie. Considering the latest theory that Haverstrum had somehow taken ranunculin, Edna felt encouraged that Rosie might help throw some new light on her husband's death. If so, Edna might then be able to figure out a motivation behind the botany professor's death. She'd planned the day's outing because she wanted to speak with Lettie first. She needed to be more circumspect with a nine-year old than someone in her thirties. Edna hadn't yet decided how she would broach the topic with either Lettie or Rosie when she pulled up before her son's home.

Edna was delighted by the reception she received from the two girls when she walked into the house. Not only her granddaughter, but Lettie, too, ran up to greet her with a hug and a huge smile.

"Whose car?" Amanda asked, turning to her mother while still bouncing with excitement.

"We'll take mine. Why don't you girls go get your coats and meet us in the garage," Irene said.

Once the girls were out of earshot, Edna said, "What's up with you watching Lettie?"

Irene gave her a strained smile. "I have no idea. Rosie phoned yesterday morning in a near panic. She had planned to take Lettie to work with her, but the child refused to get dressed. When Rosie called, she was already late for work and thought she might lose her job. She asked if I'd take Lettie for the day. Since Rosie had to leave right away, I took Amanda over to their house. Rosie left while we waited for Lettie to get ready. She was totally cooperative once her mother was gone. Then we came back here. Last night, when Rosie came to pick up her daughter, we had a little talk. Long and short of it is that Lettie is happier playing with Amanda until they go back to school."

"That's pretty strange behavior and a defiance I didn't think Lettie had in her."

"Me either," Irene agreed.

Figuring the girls might be coming to check on the old slowpokes, Edna quickly told Irene of her wish to get Lettie alone for as long as possible. "I'd like to ask her some sensitive questions, and I think she's more apt to talk to me if nobody else is in the room."

"We should be able to manage that," Irene said over her shoulder as she reached into the closet for her own coat and handbag. She then hooked her arm through Edna's and led her through the kitchen and out to the garage.

At the Warwick Mall, after hitting nearly every store from Macy's to Penny's to Target, Irene and Edna sagged gratefully into a booth, happy to finally get off their feet. The girls sat opposite and put their heads together over a menu, arguing good-naturedly over whether to get pizza or a burger, and then what toppings were best. Edna and Irene thought the half sandwich and cup of soup looked most appealing. As yet, Edna hadn't had a chance to speak with Lettie alone.

The opportunity came after they returned home and settled around the kitchen table.

"Will you braid my hair?" As Amanda pulled her purchases from a bag with the Target logo, she looked up at her mother with pleading eyes.

Glancing swiftly at Edna and giving a nearly imperceptible nod toward Lettie, Irene said, "Sure, kiddo, but first let's go up to the bathroom and I'll give you a professional shampoo."

"Cool," Amanda said, jumping up to follow her mother out of the room.

Sitting at the head of the rectangular table with Lettie on the side to her left, Edna began to help arrange nail polish and manicure implements. The girls had bought some new colors during their morning's shopping. At the advice of the woman behind the perfume counter, auburn-headed Amanda had chosen a metallic red and blonde Lettie a glittery pink.

"I think your mother will like the color you picked," Edna said as she picked up an emery board. She held a palm out and Lettie obligingly placed her own hand in Edna's.

Keeping her eyes on their hands, Lettie shrugged.

As Edna began to file the girl's ragged fingernails into shape, she knew she didn't have much time to get a nine-year-old talking. She hoped a gentle but aggressive approach would work. "Why didn't you want to go to work with her? Planning weddings must be lots of fun."

Again, the girl merely shrugged and kept her eyes lowered.

"Do you know what sort of things she does?" Edna was getting desperate. Would the girl ever speak?

This time, only one arm went up and Lettie's head tipped sideways so shoulder and ear nearly touched. "I dunno. She doesn't let me help. It's boring just watching."

Edna raised her eyes in surprise and looked at the girl. "I think you'd be a good helper."

"Me, too."

"What do you do, if she won't let you help?" Edna returned her gaze to the girl's fingers as she finished with the right and accepted the left one.

Lettie shook her head slightly, but this time, she looked up at Edna. "I read."

Edna was at a loss and worked silently for nearly a minute. She didn't want to get off on a discussion of preferred stories. She was about to see if she could get

Lettie to talk about her grandmother when the girl surprised her by saying, "Mama's different."

Careful, Edna thought before asking nonchalantly. "What do you mean?"

"She used to be happy before Daddy died. At least, some of the time."

Edna was anxious to say the right thing so the girl would keep talking.

"Do you miss your daddy?"

Lettie nodded and dropped her gaze to the nails Edna was gently filing. The fingers of the girl's right hand were smoothing the dish towel with which Irene had covered the wood surface.

"You were pretty young when he died. Do you remember him?"

Lettie nodded. "I have his picture on my dresser."

"That's nice. I bet that helps to keep him in your dreams at night."

Lettie looked up in surprise, as if Edna were clairvoyant. "It does." She seemed to study Edna for several seconds while Edna herself pretended to assess the girl's hands with approval. Her heart beat rapidly, hoping Lettie would keep talking.

"What did your daddy look like?"

"He could have been a movie star."

Edna almost smiled, but the awe in the child's voice kept her from doing so. She didn't want Lettie to think she was being laughed at.

"He got sick."

Lettie sounded so forlorn, Edna had to clear a lump in her throat before speaking again. "Yes, I know he did. Do you know what made him sick?"

Lettie shook her head, while her eyes examined the bottles of polish. "Lily's medicine didn't make him better."

At that moment, Amanda burst into the kitchen with Irene close behind. "Have you painted yet? Did you wait for me?" Her hair was soft and shiny from the recent wash and blow drying.

Edna wanted to beat her head on the table in frustration. She needed more time alone with the girl. Thinking back to the morning Starling had driven them to Point Judith and Lettie's mention of "Lily's medicine," Edna wondered if Lettie had just referred to the same concoction she'd spoken of when the girls had been looking at Edna's sketch of the Christmas Rose.

Any more chance of getting Lettie alone disappeared with the arrival of Irene's three older children. The noise level in the kitchen increased as grandchildren greeted Edna. Allison sat across the table from Lettie to examine the polish while David and Joseph raided the refrigerator.

"What's for supper?" David asked as he put a carton of milk on the countertop and reached into a cupboard for a glass.

"Spaghetti," Irene said, "so don't spoil your appetites."

"As if," Allison murmured and rolled her eyes. In a lower tone, she said, "Can I make the sauce?"

"You bet," Irene agreed with a grin as she finished off Amanda's braid with a rubber band. Dropping into organizer mode, she said, "The girls need to finish painting their nails. As soon as the polish is dry, I want Amanda and Lettie to set the table. Since Allison is helping cook, you boys are in charge of cleanup tonight." She had to raise her voice on those last words as she spoke to the backs of David and Joseph who, with a box of cookies and the carton of milk, were heading for the family room in the basement.

In a lower tone, talking to those who remained in the room, she said, "I'll make garlic bread and I bet we can talk Gramma into whipping up a peach cobbler."

"Yeah," Amanda nearly shouted. "Will you, Gramma?"

Edna smiled. "How can I refuse?"

The meal proceeded with much chatter and laughter, followed by two simultaneous groans when Irene reminded the boys that they were on kitchen patrol.

Rosie had not appeared by the time Edna was ready to head home at eight o'clock that night. Once alone in the quiet of her car, her thoughts returned to Lettie's words, "Lily's medicine didn't make him better."

Had the child, then seven years old, given her father what she thought was medicine her grandmother had prepared? Had the youngster seen Lily administer it to Gregory? What exactly had Lettie meant by that seemingly simple statement?

Chapter 19

Edna found two new messages on her office machine when she arrived home shortly before nine that evening. Family and friends who knew her well had learned to rely on her land line. She reserved her cell mainly for emergencies or for connecting with someone at an airport or train station. Otherwise, the instrument was apt to be left in the car or in her purse or, worse yet, needing to be recharged. Besides, she informed the uninitiated, she preferred to listen to calls in the uninterrupted quiet of her office.

Having grown up in a generation before computers were as necessary to daily life as televisions, Edna prohibited electronic devices at the dinner table or when the family was gathered to enjoy each other's company. Absolutely no mobile calls were accepted when she was driving, shopping or visiting. She relied on voice mail to help her manage her day without endless or inconvenient disruptions.

Albert had phoned at five that evening to tell her they would be out on the boat with cellular reception unpredictable. She took that to mean he may or may not turn on his mobile. He went on to say that the weather was near-perfect, as were ocean conditions, so they were going to enjoy another peaceful night at sea. He assured her he was doing fine, and hoped she was finding time to relax and catch up on her reading while he was away. She felt only a small pang of guilt over this last thought.

Preferring not to dwell on this feeling, she concentrated instead on regrets over missing a chance to speak with her husband. She was happy to know the trip was going well, and hoped it would help Albert's rehabilitation, although she wasn't certain if he would get sufficient exercise for his knee on board a cabin cruiser. Sighing with resignation over what was out of her control, she listened to the next call.

"Edna, it's Tuck. Call me when you get this, please, no matter the time. We need to talk."

Tuck must have been waiting near the phone because she picked up on the first ring. "We have to do something about Peppa," she said after she and Edna exchanged brief preliminary greetings.

"What do you mean?"

"She just sits by the phone, waiting for word. I have no idea when Clem's autopsy results will be in, but she isn't doing herself any good by moping around the house. Knowing her, I bet she's imagining the worst."

Edna thought for a minute before a plan came to mind. "Why don't you bring her here for breakfast tomorrow morning? Tell her to bring Rufus. I'll ask my neighbor to join us. She'll bring Hank, her Labrador. If introducing the two dogs doesn't distract Peppa, I don't know what will."

"Who's your neighbor?" Tuck asked.

"Mary Osbourne. I don't know if you two have met, but she grew up here so she must have been one of Peppa's Saturday morning kids. She's a bit of a distraction herself." Edna was certain that Mary's ghost theories would provide another diversion for Peppa.

Tuck sounded skeptical but agreed. "I suppose that will do for an hour or so, if I can persuade Peppa to leave the house. Afterwards, though, I'm afraid she'll go right back home to brood."

"Maybe we can take care of that, too. Between now and then, I'll ring Charlie and find out if he's heard anything," Edna said, ending the call. Before she phoned the detective, however, she dialed Mary's number.

"Sure, I know Peppa." Edna could hear the delight in Mary's voice as she accepted the invitation to breakfast. The pleasure vanished with her next words, though. "I was sorry to hear about the professor. I didn't even know he'd moved back to town when I heard he'd been run over by his ex-wife. Is it true?" Always on the alert for the latest news around town, Mary was probably hoping to pump Edna for more details.

"Yes and no," said Edna, purposely vague. "When you see her tomorrow, please don't mention it. She's upset enough over what happened, and we want to take her mind off it for a while. Besides bringing Hank with you, I was thinking you could tell them about your ghost."

The silence that followed this request lasted so long that Edna thought perhaps Mary had hung up. She was about to speak when Mary said in a near whisper, "It's not a runaway slave."

Edna gave an inward sigh and wondered what was coming next. "You've been reading more history?" She made the statement sound like a question, knowing Mary would explain without even that much encouragement.

"Not exactly. I found something. Tell you about it at breakfast. The ghost is the spirit of someone who knew my grandfather. Makes sense, too. I bet Father knew this guy was haunting the house and didn't want to scare Mother. Nanny would have moved out, if she'd had any idea there was an unseen presence in the nursery." Mary chuckled. "That risk alone would have been enough for Father to keep anything supernatural under wraps."

Edna nearly laughed aloud as she thought of what Mary would have been like as a child, and Mr. Osbourne's terror that he and his wife might be left in complete charge of their precocious offspring. A whirling dervish around her elderly parents, Edna was certain. "Do I get a hint?"

"Rather tell you in person," was Mary's curt reply.

Edna still thought the entire idea of a ghost was pretty far-fetched, but Mary sounded too serious for Edna to make light of her neighbor's notion. She would wait to hear the latest flight of fancy, but she believed that the real culprit must be a bird or an animal or the wind.

After finishing her call to Mary, Edna rang Charlie's mobile. To her amazement, he picked up almost at once.

"Not busy?" she asked.

"Tonight's been quiet. I'm wrapping up some paperwork before heading home. I can use an early night."

Surprised that he was still in the office, Edna quickly reconsidered merely speaking to him on the phone. "Have you eaten today?"

Charlie laughed. "Is that why you called?"

She didn't directly answer his question. "Since you aren't already comfortably ensconced at home, why don't you swing by here first? I'll fix something for you to eat, and I'm thinking you wouldn't turn down a nightcap."

"You're right about that." He paused, then said almost accusingly. "That's not all, is it?"

"No," she said. "I want to hear whatever you can tell me about Clem Peppafitch, and I'd rather hear it in the coziness of my living room with a glass of wine in my hand. "

Forty-five minutes later, Charlie was sitting on the couch across the coffee table from Edna. She'd grilled ham-and-cheese sandwiches and added homemade oatmeal-raisin cookies to his plate. Knowing he'd prefer something stronger than a glass of wine, she raided Albert's whiskey and vermouth supply to fix the detective a manhattan.

She made small talk while Charlie quenched his thirst and took the edge off his hunger. When he finally put the plate on the coffee table and settled back with the rest of his drink, she asked the question foremost on her mind. "Have you heard anything from the medical examiner about Clem?"

"I hadn't before you phoned tonight," Charlie said, "but after you mentioned it, I thought I'd contact someone I know who works in the lab."

"And ..." she prompted when he stopped talking to sip his drink. She suspected he was teasing her by dragging out the suspense.

"Digitalis overdose."

It was so sudden and unexpected an answer that she didn't think she'd heard correctly. "What?"

"So far, it looks like he died of a drug overdose," Charlie repeated. He frowned. "They're still waiting for the complete toxicology screens, but it's fairly certain that the poor old guy was dead before he was run over. Peppa didn't kill him with her car. It was unfortunate and simple coincidence that he collapsed across her driveway."

"Do you really believe in that much of a coincidence?"

Charlie shrugged. "Hard to say until the investigation is over. Peggy King is the lead detective on this one. Patrol's been going house-to-house, asking if anyone saw what happened Saturday night. One rookie found a neighbor just this morning who corroborated another neighbor's story about a man stumbling in the direction of Peppa's house shortly before ten Saturday night. This new witness had turned off the downstairs lights before going upstairs to bed when she noticed it was snowing, so she put on a coat and went out to call in her cat. That's when she saw what she described as 'an old drunk weaving his way up the street.' He was 'three sheets to the wind' with his head down and shoulders hunched, so the witness said she hadn't recognized him. That sighting was about a half hour before Peppa said she got home." Charlie rattled the ice in his glass, watching the liquid swirl. "Could have been too much medication combined with booze that did him in, I suppose."

Edna thought for a minute or two while she sipped her wine and stared into the fire. Charlie was quiet, too, seemingly waiting for her to tell him what was on her mind.

"According to Tuck," Edna began, speaking her thoughts aloud and turning to look at the detective, "Clem Peppafitch had been sober for several years. We think he came back to town to make up with Peppa, so it doesn't make sense that he'd fall off the wagon."

"What are you thinking?" Charlie frowned at her.

"That there could be reasons other than alcohol that Clem was staggering or reeling or whatever it was he was doing to look as if he were drunk."

Charlie shrugged but nodded. "What would you guess?"

"I don't know." Edna looked down into her own glass for a few seconds before pushing the question to the back of her mind. Gazing back at Charlie, she asked, "Why didn't that person come forward Sunday morning? Surely everyone on the block must have seen or talked about all the police activity at Peppa's house."

Charlie looked at her with a raised eyebrow as if surprised she would ask. "People seldom want to get involved. Some wait and hope the police won't come knocking on their door. When we do track them down, they still don't always admit to something they saw or overheard."

Edna switched the conversation back again to Clem himself and shook her head in sadness. "I'm sorry if he was drinking again. I'd have thought he'd stay sober if he wanted to win Peppa back, if that really was his purpose in moving back to town, as Tuck suspects."

"Now that you've brought it up," Charlie said, leaning forward to set his glass on the coffee table. "I don't remember hearing anyone at the scene mention anything about booze. I'll check that out tomorrow with the M.E.'s office. See if they found alcohol in his blood and, if so, how much. I'll talk to Peggy King and John Forrester, too. They were both at the scene Sunday morning, close to the body. Either of them would have noticed if Clem had been drinking. Someone drunk enough to be unsteady on his feet would have reeked of the stuff."

Edna didn't want to think about John Forrester, so she changed the subject. "I'm relieved for Peppa. It must be bad enough to have run over her ex-husband, so I don't know what it would have done to her if she were responsible for his death. When will you tell her?"

"Since it's Detective King's case, I called her after talking to my lab friend. She was tucked up at home but said she'd go over and see Peppa. Peggy's another of the Saturday morning story kids, you know. She was glad for the chance to ease Peppa's mind a little." He grinned at Edna before adding more soberly, "Until all the test results are in, about the only thing we can do is inform Peppa that it wasn't her car that killed Clem." He turned his wrist to look at his watch. "I imagine Peggy's giving Peppa the news right about now."

Chapter 20

Wednesday morning, Tuck and Peppa drove up shortly after nine o'clock in Tuck's big blue Lincoln town car. Edna quickly put on her coat and boots and went out to greet them. It was true that she had asked Mary to bring Hank over, thinking that introducing the two dogs would be a nice distraction for the librarian, but that didn't mean she wanted the two dogs greeting each other for the first time inside her house.

The retired librarian looked better, but not nearly back to her former self. Tuck, however, was absolutely bubbling. She had gotten out and was shutting the driver's side door as Edna came out of the house.

"Good news, isn't it, Edna?" she burbled as Peppa pushed herself out of the passenger seat.

Edna, nearing the vehicle as Peppa stood, heard the librarian mumble, "He's still dead," as she pulled a blue knit cap snugly onto her tight gray curls. "Wasn't digitalis," she said in a firmer voice, looking Edna straight in the eye. "Told that to Peggy last night."

"But you've been cleared. You are not to blame," argued Tuck, coming around the hood to stand beside her friends. "Don't you feel better about that?"

Instead of answering, Peppa reached to open the back door. Rufus's head emerged, and she attached a lead to his collar before allowing him to jump down onto the driveway.

Edna was confused. Ignoring Tuck, she spoke to Peppa. "Last night, Charlie told me Clem died of an overdose of digitalis. Do you know something different?"

At that moment, Rufus, tail wagging, looked beyond Edna toward the back yard and gave a single sharp bark, as if to say "Good morning."

The women all turned to see Mary slogging across the yard in calf-deep snow, following Hank who was bounding toward the group, his own tail wagging furiously. Distracted from her conversation with Peppa, Edna gasped, wondering if Hank were about to lunge at Rufus. She thought the bigger Rottweiler would clearly come out the victor. He was at least twenty or thirty pounds heavier than the smaller lab, clearly more muscle than fat. She was beginning to panic, wondering what to do if a fight broke out, when she heard Peppa call delightedly, "Hank? Hank, is that you?"

Turning to ask "You know Hank?" Edna saw Peppa bend down and remove the leash from Rufus's collar.

"Of course" said Peppa. "Tom Greene used to bring Hank along whenever he did handy work for me. Hank and Rufus were great friends. After Tom died, I heard someone had adopted the Lab, but I had no idea Hank's new owner was your next-door neighbor. If I had, I would have brought Rufus over to visit sooner."

As they talked, Edna watched the two dogs. At first they had run up to each other, sniffing and wiggling happily. Suddenly Hank raced several yards away and spun to face Rufus. Dropping his head and shoulders, Hank waited for the big dog to accept the challenge. It took Rufus only seconds before he ran forward to leap onto the younger, friskier dog. Before Rufus landed on him, however, the black Lab jumped sideways, causing the Rottweiler to skid past.

"Let the games begin," Peppa shouted and laughed, clapping her hands. And indeed the games did begin with Hank prancing around the bigger dog and then taking off as fast as the snow would allow, around the south side of the house to the backyard. After a slight hesitation, Rufus took off after him. Several seconds later, the women watched as the two dogs came back into view and raced toward the stone wall that bordered the south side of the Davies property.

After watching the canine antics for several minutes, Mary strolled closer to the small group of older women. "I guess they know each other, huh?" she said, thrusting her hands deep into the pockets of her thick green-and-brown camo jacket. "I remember you from story hour at the library."

"Of course, you're Mary Osborne. I remember you as quite an outspoken young lady." Peppa grinned up at Mary with a twinkle in her blue-gray eyes.

Edna, always amazed that Mary seemed to show up at exactly the right moment, noticed that Peppa was beginning to look more her old self. That thought brought Edna back to Peppa's earlier comment about the circumstances of Clem's death. She need to ask about that, but not standing out in the cold morning air. "Shall we go in? I've a fresh pot of coffee brewing."

"I'm ready," Tuck spoke up, rubbing her hands up and down her upper arms. "I haven't had a drop yet this morning."

Mary whistled for Hank. Obediently, he stopped wrestling with Rufus and came running. Since the Rottweiler was right on the Lab's heels, Peppa didn't need to call her own dog. Edna led the way down the brick path, recently shoveled by the Benton brothers, and the back door to the mudroom.

When everyone had shed coats, hats, boots and gloves, and the canines had been toweled off, Edna turned and saw Benjamin sitting nonchalantly in the doorway to the kitchen. Smiling to herself, she knew her cat was up to something. Sure enough, the black Lab walked jauntily into the kitchen past the ginger cat. The massive Rottweiler, hurrying after his friend until he spied the feline, decided his best course of action was to back up and stand still until his mistress came to rescue him.

Having taken off her coat, Tuck reached for Peppa's and draped them both on the seat of the nearby parson's bench. She then placed a hand between Peppa's shoulder blades and propelled her gently toward the kitchen with Rufus following meekly behind. Benjamin, his point made, preceded them with slow, dignified steps as if he were leading a parade.

"Something smells wonderful, Edna," Tuck said. "What have you made for us?"

"I thought a spinach quiche would taste good. Cantaloupe and apple-cinnamon muffins to begin."

"Yum." Tuck sat at the kitchen table next to Peppa and reached for the bread basket as Edna poured coffee. Mary took the chair opposite her old story-hour host.

Rufus settled on the floor between Tuck and Peppa after Benjamin jumped silently onto a chair against the wall, where he commanded a view of the room. As was his habit, Hank dropped down in front of the cat's perch and laid his head on paws, ready for a nap.

"Are you working this morning?" Edna said to Mary, cutting the quiche and serving her guests. She noticed once her neighbor had removed the jacket, Mary wasn't in her usual casual attire, but wearing plain white slacks and a mint green tunic.

"Doin' a favor for one of the other hospital volunteers," was all Mary offered before reaching for a warm muffin.

The next twenty minutes or so seemed to Edna to drag as she tried to hold up a cheerful conversation with some help from Tuck. Despite the pleasant distraction of the dogs' reunion, Peppa seemed to withdraw back into her own thoughts, and Mary seemed tense with suppressed excitement. When, at last, the meal was over, plates cleared away and coffee mugs refilled, Mary spoke to Edna.

"Can I tell 'em about my ghost now?"

Before Edna could answer, Tuck piped up. "Ghosts?"

That was all the encouragement Mary needed. "Yup. A smuggler. Ran whiskey down the coast during Prohibition."

Edna nearly choked on the sip of coffee she'd just taken. She should know better than to take a drink as Mary was about to drop a bombshell. "So you've definitely decided it isn't a runaway slave?"

Mary shook her head, her green eyes glittering with enthusiasm. "Not since I found the letter written to my grandfather."

"You found an old letter?" Peppa's interest had been sparked, and Edna remembered Tuck mentioning that the librarian was an avid student of local history and folklore.

"Yup," Mary nodded. "In a book of my grandpa's."

"I love reading old letters," Peppa said, leaning forward to rest clasped hands on the table. "What does yours say? Did you bring it with you?"

Mary shook her head. "It's too brittle and a piece is missing. It's tearing at the fold, so I put it back in the book."

Hiding a smile behind her napkin as she dabbed at her mouth, Edna thought Mary might also be dangling it to entice them all to her house so she could persuade them to help her hunt down this phantom of hers.

"What's it about, this letter you found?" The new topic had obviously brought Peppa out of the doldrums.

"Like I said, it was written to my grandfather. There's a piece missing, and the ink is smudged in one spot. Looks like something spilled on it, but the gist is still there. What I make out is that it introduced a man named Sam Hopkins and asked Grandpa to hide him if he ever showed up on the doorstep. Seems Sam was the son of the reverend who wrote to Grandpa. Because of his smuggling activities--which, apparently, were okay with his reverent papa--Sam was hiding from organized crime bosses as well as revenuers. He had to stay away from the family home in Newport."

Peppa nodded. "Many church elders felt the law to ban alcohol was both un-American and un-Christian. Makes sense. Rhode Island and Connecticut were the only two states not to ratify the Eighteenth Amendment to the Constitution. Rhode Island was about the most anti-prohibition state in the country." Her expression became sad and thoughtful, making Edna wonder if Peppa were thinking of Clem and his problem with alcohol.

"I heard that, too," Tuck spoke into the silence when Peppa didn't go on. "Rhode Island's four hundred miles of coastline with hundreds of inlets, coves and small islands has always been a smuggler's paradise. During the Roaring Twenties, local rumrunners went all the way to Canada to get hard liquor--what they called 'the real stuff,'' while revenuers in other states contended only with mere beer and bathtub-gin bootleggers."

Mary nodded, clearly enjoying the response her story was generating. "Grandpa had a walking stick with a glass tube in the center. Father once told me that Grandpa called it his lemonade cane and carried it whenever he went anywhere with his gentlemen friends."

Peppa seemed to revive slightly as she smiled at Mary's memory. "Do you still have the cane?"

"Sure do. It's in the umbrella stand by the front door. I'll show it to you. The letter, too," Mary said, pushing her chair back from the table.

"Wait," Edna said, laying a restraining hand on Mary's forearm before she could rise. "What makes you think this Sam what's-his-name is your ghost?"

Mary's eyes sparkled. "I think the smudge on the letter is blood. I bet he was hurt and came to Grandpa for help."

"Would your grandfather have put the rest of his

family in jeopardy by harboring a fugitive?" Tuck asked with a shiver. "I wouldn't have wanted to mess with the mob, back then. I remember reading about Frank Morelli and Raymond Patriarca and some of the other local gangsters from the Roaring Twenties. From what I've read, they were mean and dangerous."

Seeming happy to explain her theory further while excusing her grandfather of any thoughtlessness on his part, Mary said, "The house was built with hidey-holes when it was a depot on the Underground Railroad." She glanced up at the kitchen clock and her face fell. "I'm gonna be late for my shift." Edna could almost see the plan forming in her neighbor's mind when Mary paused briefly. "Will you come to my house tonight, Peppa?" she said, sliding a quick glance at Edna. "I can show you Grandpa's cane and the false chimney and maybe we might even see my ghost."

Edna was certain Mary was inviting Peppa so that Edna would join them in a late-night mystical adventure.

Chapter 21

As her breakfast guests drove away, Edna mused over what she'd just gotten roped into. Peppa had agreed to be at Mary's house about the time the late-night news aired. Tuck had been so pleased that Peppa was acting like her old self, that she, too, said she would join them. Edna, feeling it would be a dubious but fun escapade, declared she wouldn't miss it for the world.

Needing to get on with her day, she put aside thoughts of the evening ahead and went to her office to check for e-mail messages. As she was waiting for the computer to boot up, she realized she hadn't had a chance to ask Peppa about her comment that Clem wouldn't have taken digitalis. What would have made her so certain when she hadn't seen him in over five years?

Finding nothing of particular interest in her mailbox, she turned to her notes on the investigation into the death of Gregory Haverstrum. *Am I getting anywhere?* Flipping through the pages of the notebook she pulled from her tote bag, she scanned what she had written. Plenty of questions, but what did she actually know?

I am quite certain that Gregory was poisoned by the toxin produced by the Christmas Rose. It would account for the strange burning around his mouth. The poison probably dissipated in the body, but symptoms remained.

Turning to a clean page in the book, she began to jot down what details she knew about the case. If he had been poisoned, then logic told her the murderer had to have been one of the visitors to his apartment the day he died. Listing their names, she realized the only person with whom she hadn't yet spoken was Bobbi Callahan.

Edna was determined to make some headway with her investigation before the sun set that day. She'd wasted enough time. Friday was Valentine's Day. Albert, Matthew and the Marlstone men would be flying home that afternoon, and she figured that would be a good time to call it quits. With that thought, she wondered if she were simply frustrated over what she felt was spinning her wheels. Disturbed as she was about the plight of Rosie and her daughter, Edna could do only so much to help, but could she stop nosing around while there were still so many unanswered questions? At that moment, she felt again the angst of being the prime suspect in another person's murder and the shame of being shunned not only by neighbors but also by those she'd considered friends. The urge to assist the Becks resurfaced with a sharpness that stunned her.

With renewed energy, she reviewed her notes in an attempt to locate Bobbi Callahan. Edna recalled that one of the stories mentioned the young woman moving back into her parents' home at the start of the initial investigation. Reporters had prowled the campus looking for her, hanging out around the dorm and library, disturbing her sleep, her study time, and her social life.

Since the Callahans' house was Bobbi's last reported residence, Edna decided that was as good a place as any to start tracking down the young woman who had been Gregory's personal assistant and suspected lover. First, Edna needed to come up with a plausible reason for wanting to locate the graduating student. She doubted either parent would give their daughter's whereabouts away just for the asking. Pulling up the LinkedIn information Bobbi had posted, Edna learned about her interest in child psychology and her plans to continue graduate studies in the field while she worked as an elementary school teacher. An idea struck Edna as soon as she noted that one of Bobbi's undergraduate papers had been published a year before, a singular achievement for the young woman. The subject of the piece was the psychological impact of peer-group rejection on adolescents.

Perfect, Edna thought, amazed at the coincidence. Excitedly optimistic, she used the Google search engine to find a local address and phone number for Duke and Louise Callahan with "other relatives" listed as Bobbi Jean. Edna's call was picked up on the fourth ring by a woman announcing herself.

"This is Louise Callahan." The voice held a pleasant confidence.

"Mrs. Callahan, my name is Edna Davies. I'd like to speak with your daughter, if she's available." Edna thought she might as well try a direct approach and avoid any dissembling, if possible.

Louise's tone turned cool and wary when she said, "May I know what this is about?"

Edna sighed inwardly. She hadn't wanted to

mislead, but she was ready with her excuse. When she spoke, she thought she sounded firm and professional. "I have friends at the university …" *Not a lie*, thought Edna. "and I understand that Bobbi has earned honors in the child psychology department." Another truth, although it was something Edna had recently read in the LinkedIn blurb, not from a college connection. Using the key component she'd learned from Bobbi's posting, Edna went on. "I understand that your daughter has done research on the effects of rejection on children. It is on that subject I wish to consult with your daughter."

Sounding more receptive, Louise said, "Oh, yes. Have you read her paper? Are you a child psychologist yourself?"

Edna felt a mother who had raised four children would probably qualify as such, but said, "No. I'm mainly concerned with the problems of a particular nine-year-old girl. I believe Bobbi has the necessary experience to assist me." *True enough*, Edna assured herself. She hoped a mother's pride would take over and Louise would be only too happy to promote her daughter's talents and interests.

"Well," said the woman on the other end of the line, sounding almost enthusiastic. Edna's heart leapt for an instant before Louise continued. "I'll give her your message. If you leave your number, I can have her call you."

"It's important that I speak with her as soon as possible. Is she at home? May I drop by sometime today? Any time. I don't think it will take long, but I'd rather not discuss the matter over the phone."

There was silence on the line for several seconds

before Louise said, "Hold a moment, please."

Nearly five minutes later, she was back. "How soon can you be here? Bobbi has to leave for campus in an hour, but if you can arrive before then, she'll be glad to help in whatever way she can."

"I'll be there shortly."

Donning her green tweed winter coat, Edna set off and was parked on the street in front of the Callahan house in a quarter of an hour. The structure was of fairly modern design compared to many other homes in the area, and sat on about three acres of land. Edna thought the building was probably no more than twenty years old. As she walked up the slightly winding cement path to the front door, she noticed that the expansive front lawn was well tended. The snow had melted enough on this southern exposure to reveal wide flower borders spread with straw beneath the large windows of what Edna thought might be a warm and bright living room.

The front door was a heavy wooden affair with an ornate stained-glass window set into the top half. Louise Callahan answered the chiming doorbell almost at once. An attractive platinum blonde in her early fifties, she greeted Edna politely.

"Good morning, Mrs. Davies."

"Edna. Please call me Edna."

"And I'm Louise," the woman replied, taking Edna's proffered hand briefly with a firm grasp of her own. "Won't you come in? Bobbi will be down in a few minutes. A friend is calling for her, so I'm afraid she can't spare much time this morning, but you did say it was urgent."

Louise Callahan was such a pleasant and seemingly

naïve woman that Edna felt her stomach begin to roil at the thought of deceiving her. Edna made up her mind that, come what may, she'd lay her cards on the table.

Following the woman into a room to the left of the entryway, Edna saw with pleasure that she'd been correct about the front room being sunny and warm. It was larger than she'd expected. The house must extend quite a way to the back, she thought, spying an almost equally large dining room beyond the living area. A few inches of pine were visible from double doors that slid into the wall either side of the opening between the two rooms. The décor confirmed in Edna's mind Duke Callahan's reputation as a wealthy entrepreneur.

Someone in the family obviously enjoyed flowers, too. Two dozen red roses sat in a vase on a side table and three purple orchids floated in a crystal bowl on the low table in front of a chintz-covered sofa. Edna could see another vase of mixed blooms on the long mahogany dining table that was surrounded by twelve matching chairs. What she could see of the house was elegant but homey. She felt comfortable and welcomed as Louise asked for her coat.

"You have a lovely home," Edna said, handing the woman the tweed garment. She declined the offer of something to drink, feeling doubly guilty at Louise's hospitality.

As Edna took a seat on the sofa, a young woman hurried into the room. She wore gray woolen slacks with a blue sweater. Her hair was pulled back and tied with a patterned silk scarf at the nape of her neck. With her blondeness and dark brown eyes, she looked as Louise must have, thirty years earlier. There could be no mistaking the relationship between these two.

"Mrs. Davies?" Bobbi came forward, offering her hand. Even her voice was much like her mother's. "I'm Bobbi Callahan. Mother said you think I can help you with a problem." She backed up to sit on the broad arm of the overstuffed chair her mother had taken across the low table from Edna. "I'm afraid I don't have much time. My ride to school will be here soon, but if you can give me a brief synopsis of the issue, I'll try to be of some assistance."

Edna would have smiled at the student's obvious academic vocabulary, if she hadn't been worried over how the two Callahan women would take her next words. She cleared her throat, knowing the dryness to be a sign of how nervous she was, took a deep breath and confessed. "The child I'm concerned about is Lettie Beck." Edna paused, realizing she still didn't know which name Rosie used for her daughter. "Or, Violet Haverstrum, as you may have known her." Noticing the shock on both women's faces and Louise leaning forward about to rise, Edna rushed on. "There really is a problem. Please hear me out."

As she described the plight of Gregory Haverstrum's wife and daughter, she saw the Callahan women's expressions change from anger to interest. Bobbi seemed to be slightly sympathetic, but only slightly. It was when Edna explained how she'd gotten involved through her daughter-in-law and granddaughter and how Amanda had befriended Lettie that she saw actual sadness and compassion appear on Bobbi's face.

When Edna ended by explaining how she'd come to the certainty that Gregory had ingested ranunculin, a plant-based poison, Louise interrupted her.

"What does this have to do with my daughter? You said she could help you, but what I'm hearing sounds like an accusation."

Still perched on the arm of her mother's chair, Bobbi put a hand on Louise's shoulder. "It's okay, Mother. I think Mrs. Davies has good reason to be worried about how these unresolved questions are and will be affecting Gregory's little girl." Bobbi turned her eyes back to Edna. "I met Gregory's daughter on several occasions during the time I worked for him, but they were only brief encounters. I didn't know her well, but please go on. I'm still unclear as to how I might be of any help."

"You were at Gregory Haverstrum's condominium the afternoon of the day he was believed to have died. Is that right?" At Bobbi's nod of assent, Edna began her questions about the food she'd brought, the condition of the kitchen, the man's appearance and behavior. Bobbi's answers didn't seem out of the ordinary until Edna asked, "Did you see or speak to anyone besides Gregory himself?"

"Yes," Bobbi responded as if it were nothing unusual. "His wife was coming into the building as I was going out. We didn't speak, just nodded to each other." Bobbi made a wry face. "She didn't like me." Bobbi must have realized that Edna knew Gregory had more than a passing interest in his young assistant because she rushed to explain. "It wasn't like I broke up her marriage. They were already separated, and she'd filed for divorce before I went to work for Gregory." For the first time, Bobbi fidgeted, picking at the fabric of her slacks. "The reporters made our relationship sound like one big sex scandal, but that wasn't true." Her large, brown eyes pleaded with Edna to believe her. "I was never intimate with Gregory. He was like a big brother. We were friends, is all." As she defended herself, she was sounding less like an academician and more like an emotional teenager.

Not unsympathetic with the upbraiding the young woman must have endured, still Edna wasn't interested in the details of the relationship between boss and assistant. She redirected the conversation. "I understand that several people brought food to Gregory. Was Rosie carrying anything when you saw her that afternoon?"

Bobbi shook her head. "She wasn't, or if she was, I didn't see it. I remember because I was asked that question more than once. The police and then the lawyers asked me what I brought with me and if I'd seen anyone else bringing something into Gregory's home. The only person I saw was Mrs. Haverstrum and she wasn't carrying anything but her purse."

At that moment, a car horn sounded. Bobbi stood and turned to look out toward the street. Edna had a clear view from the sofa and noticed a small, red coup pulling up behind her Buick. When Bobbi approached the wide windows and waved, the driver waved back.

As she headed to the front hall, she apologized. "I'm sorry, but I have to go or Kisha and I will both be late for class. I don't think I've been much help, but I really don't know what else I can tell you."

Edna was discouraged at learning little more than she already knew, but stood to shake the young woman's hand. "You've been very kind and patient with me. Thank you for your time." She added with a smile, "And good luck with your career."

Once Bobbi disappeared from the room, Edna returned to the sofa for her tote bag. Louise was standing, obviously waiting to escort Edna to the door, when a question popped out of Edna's mouth, completely unexpected. Later, she was to wonder what made her ask.

"Do you know a detective named John Forrester?"

Louise's face flushed as she groped for the chair and nearly fell backwards onto the seat. "Why are you asking about John? What has he to do with this?"

"That's what I'd like to know. Do you know he was originally assigned to lead the investigation into Gregory Haverstrum's death and then removed the very next day?" Louise nodded, catching Edna off guard. "You do?" Then recovering herself quickly, she said, "Do you know why?"

The woman nodded again, not taking her eyes from Edna's. "When Duke heard that Bobbi was a major player in the investigation, he went straight to the police chief and insisted John be taken off the case." Louise was wringing her hands now, shaking her head. "There was a conflict of interest. You see, John is Bobbi's father."

Chapter 22

The news hit Edna like a strong ocean wave. She sank back heavily onto the sofa. Many questions buzzed in her head, but what finally came out of her mouth was, "Does Bobbi know?"

Louise nodded. "Oh yes. She was five when Duke adopted her. I've never hidden anything from her. I didn't initiate talks about her biological father, but whenever she had questions about him, I tried to answer as honestly as I could. Then, John looked us up when he moved to town four years ago. I got the feeling he was very proud of himself for appearing on our doorstep, unexpected and unannounced. He had the biggest grin on his face, as if to say, 'I'm a whole lot smarter than you.' But, so far, I've had the last laugh." She scrunched up her nose in a smug expression. "My husband is an old boyhood friend of the police chief."

"Do you mind talking about John?" Edna didn't know why but she felt she had stumbled onto an important piece of the puzzle she was trying to assemble. "I've bumped into him several times this past week, since I've been trying to help young Lettie. I'm uncertain what he's after. I'd like to know more about him, what sort of person he is."

"Maybe you'd like some coffee while we talk," Louise Callahan said. "I know I can use a cup." As she took Edna's arm and walked her to the back of the house, she added, "I feel more relaxed in my kitchen, don't you?"

While Louise began brewing a fresh pot, Edna stood before double-wide glass doors, looking out onto a flagstone patio and beyond to a large, irregularly shaped swimming pool surrounded by a cement apron. Raised beds dotted the remainder of a generous expanse of yard that was enclosed by a wooden privacy fence, along which stood trellises for climbing vines. The snow had melted from most of the gravel between the wooden planters, and Edna could tell that weeds had no chance to take hold anywhere in this immaculate courtyard.

"The outside of your home is as lovely as the inside," Edna said, turning to face Louise.

"Thank you. Duke and I worked with an architect the first year we were married. He'd owned these three acres for several years but had never built on them. You may have noticed," she said with raised eyebrows and an amused expression, "we have an abundance of planters and pots in our enclosed half acre. Duke loves flowers of all kinds but he excels as a vegetable gardener. It's his passion. Not so much in the winter months but during the rest of the year, he's outside more than in, once he gets home from work."

"Do you and Bobbi share his passion?" Edna asked.

"I, not so much. I do some of the weeding, but Bobbi has followed Duke around, helping him tend the beds, ever since he and I were married sixteen years ago." She checked the percolator and turned back to Edna. "When the sun's out, the deck can be pleasant.

Would you like to step outside for a few minutes while the coffee brews?"

Edna was almost dizzy with new implications as the woman slid open one side of the glass wide enough for them to move onto the deck. *Duke and Bobbi were both expert gardeners, and each was associated with Gregory Haverstrum. Did they know Clem Peppafitch, as well? Duke certainly was old enough to have taken a class from the professor.* Another thought jumped into her head as she stepped out onto redwood planks, *John Forrester must know Duke Callahan is an avid gardener. Would the detective think to accuse his ex-wife's husband of murder? Why was Forrester so determined to investigate a two-year-old death?*

Shaking her head clear of these distracting ideas, Edna concentrated on the scene from the deck. She saw that the house's extension, a single story behind the two-story main building, held another set of sliding doors. These ones, however, were covered by drawn curtains.

Louise must have noticed Edna studying them because she said, "Our mother-in-law apartment behind the kitchen, at least it was until we moved my mother to an assisted living complex three years ago. We have a graduate student living with us now. She helps with the housework in exchange for free room and board. The only thing we ask is that she not entertain here." Louise hunched and rubbed her upper arms. "Brrr. It's not quite as warm as it looked. Shall we have that coffee now?"

Seated at the center island on swivel bar stools with enough padding on the seat and chair back to be comfortable, Edna returned to Louise's previous revelation. "You said your former husband looked you up when he moved to town. I take it he isn't from around here, then?"

Louise shook her head, but seemed reluctant to speak. Edna realized it was a painful subject for the woman, so she tried to think of a simple, unthreatening question. Finally, she said, "How did you meet John?"

Louise gripped the coffee mug between her hands, as if to warm them. After a brief pause, she looked across at Edna and gave a weary sigh.

"I was an emergency room nurse at a small hospital in western Massachusetts. John came in one evening with the victim of a gunshot."

When she seemed to run out of steam, Edna prompted with a wry grin, "And you fell in love with the man in uniform?"

Louise looked startled. "No," burst from her lips. "Not at all. I did not want to marry a cop. I did not want to live wondering if my husband would come home in the evening. Besides which, he had two other strikes against him, in my book. He's fifteen years older than I and had already been married twice."

Edna was confused. "Then, why …"

"He wore me down," Louise cut in. She glared at Edna for several seconds, but Edna realized the woman was not seeing her. Rather, Louise seemed to be sorting through images inside her head. Finally, her focus came back to Edna's face, but she didn't speak.

Edna decided to push a little harder. She needed answers. Reaching across the island's granite surface, she rested a hand lightly on Louise's forearm. "I promise you, I'm not a ghoulish gossip monger. Ever since I met Rosie Beck and her daughter, I've seen John hovering around. He came to my house and threatened me. Part of what I'm asking you is should I be afraid? Is he violent?"

Louise's eyes grew wide. "Oh, goodness," she exhaled. "I'm not sure. Until he showed up four years ago, I hadn't seen him for more than a decade. I wanted nothing to do with him. Didn't want to know where he was or what he was doing."

"What was he like when you did know him?" Edna asked. "He couldn't have been too mean if you married him despite his age and occupation." She smiled when she spoke, hoping to lighten the dark mood that had descended on the kitchen.

Louise smiled back weakly as if in appreciation of Edna's attempt, and the dam seemed to break. "He's a handsome man and can be very charming when he wants to be. After our first meeting, he came into the E.R. regularly, sometimes escorting a prisoner, but mostly by himself. When I'd go on a coffee break, I'd often find him waiting for me in the cafeteria. He kept asking me out and I kept refusing." She breathed deeply, shook her head as if at her own folly, and took a sip of coffee. " I finally decided to go out with him just to make him stop pestering me. Figured he'd get tired of me and go away." She looked at Edna sheepishly. "My little plan sure backfired. We were married eight months after our first date. I was twenty-three, twenty-eight when we had Bobbi."

"Five years married," Edna said. "What happened?"

Louise grimaced. "Shortly after the wedding ceremony, John turned into someone I didn't know. Besides becoming unreasonably jealous and possessive, he no longer hid a heavy drinking habit from me. He was a mean, abusive drunk." Louise must have seen the look of dismay on Edna's face because she hurriedly said, "Oh, he didn't hit me. Sometimes, I wish he had. I would have left him immediately. As it was, I think the verbal and emotional humiliation left deeper scars than any beating he could have given me. There were no obvious marks to show anyone who might listen and believe my side of things. I took it for six years, always thinking … hoping things would get better. When Bobbi was barely a year old, John started in on her. I couldn't stand by and let that happen. I didn't want her to grow up with the kind of mental insecurity that her father would have dumped on her."

Edna was curious. "He let you go? Just like that?"

Louise shook her head and sipped from her mug before replying. "I left in the middle of the night when he was on duty. Even that was risky because he used to drive by the house periodically. He never would've let me go, if he'd suspected. One of the women in the department figured out what was going on. She'd apparently been a friend of John's first wife. Actually, she was the one who convinced me that I needed to take Bobbi and get away. I packed a few days' worth of clothes for each of us and hid a borrowed suitcase in Bobbi's closet. That was about the only place I knew John would never look. I was ready for nearly two weeks and the waiting was killing me. I was so nervous, I was certain John would sense something was up. Then, my friend phoned at one in the morning on a Saturday night. Said John had just been dispatched to a bar brawl and would be tied up long enough for me to be certain

he wouldn't catch me leaving our neighborhood."
Louise's face twisted as if she were in pain. "I don't
often speak of that time. It brings back too many awful
feelings."

"So you moved to Rhode Island," Edna changed the
conversation to what she hoped would lead to happier
thoughts for the woman. "Why South County?"

Louise's features relaxed slightly. "I grew up here."
She perked up as more of her story unfolded. "My father
died when I was seven. I was an only child and Mother
never remarried, so she was delighted to have me move
back home. It worked out well for us both. I got a job at
the South County as a floor nurse on the night shift and
was able to spend days with Bobbi. I'd feed her and get
her into her pajamas before I left for work, so it wasn't
all that hard on Mother to read a bedtime story and tuck
a tired little toddler in for the night."

"Had you known Duke Callahan when you lived
here before?"

Louise shook her head. "No. I met him when he was
a patient at the hospital. He had been in a terrible, seven-
car pileup one cold, icy night. Duke was the worst hurt
of anyone and stayed in the hospital for two weeks. He
had terrible dreams and would wake up at night, unable
to get back to sleep. On many occasion, I would sit and
talk or read to him until he relaxed enough to drift off.
By the time he was well enough to be released, we had
fallen in love." Louise paused and looked into the
distance, but Edna suspected the woman wasn't seeing
anything in particular. Her face had taken on a serene
and happy expression. After several seconds, she
seemed to snap out of whatever memory had captured

her and continued with her narration. "Duke's ten years my senior but he doesn't act it. At age sixty, he's as physically fit and vital as a forty-year-old."

Louise stood and brought the coffee pot to the island. She refilled both mugs before resuming her seat.

"What about John?" Edna said. "He didn't come after you?"

Louise shook her head. "Not really surprising that he didn't. My co-conspirator in the department helped me there, too. I heard that the chief somehow got word of my having to run off in the middle of the night and why. My friend didn't tell me directly, but I'm convinced she was responsible. Happily, John never suspected her or I'm sure he would have made her life unbearable. As it was, the chief threatened to dismiss John as an abuser if he got near me. A year later, when I filed for divorce, John didn't protest."

Edna nodded in understanding. "For a cop accused of domestic violence, it would mean the end of his career," she said, adding, "He would never be able to carry a gun again."

Louise agreed and said with noticeable relief. "The chief was a good man. Made it easy for me to be free of John. And when Duke petitioned to adopt Bobbi shortly after we were married, again there wasn't a peep of protest from John."

"And you say he never struck you?" Edna was still trying to figure out if the man were capable of physical harm.

Louise shook her head. "I used to hear grumblings from people in the department that he might be unduly rough when arresting someone, but he never laid a hand on me or Bobbi. Like I said, if he had, I would have left him instantly."

"Sounds like you were lucky he didn't come after you," Edna said. "I imagine that most jealous, possessive men wouldn't give up so easily."

"Absolutely," Louise said with a roll of her eyes.

Edna knew she was outstaying her welcome, but there was another question she wanted to ask. "Why did he show up so many years later?"

Louise winced. "I have no idea. He *said* he wanted to get to know his daughter. Wanted to be part of her life." The woman shook her head in disgust. "After nearly sixteen years? I found that hard to believe, but as long as he behaves himself, I can't complain. Bobbi is old enough and smart enough to know her own mind, and Duke will see that no harm comes to her. He has been fiercely protective of Bobbi since the day he met her. Even if we hadn't married, I think he'd still watch over her." Louise's expression softened when she spoke of her current husband.

"Do they spend time together, Bobbi and John?"

"Not much. I think John is intimidated by Duke. Like all bullies, John's a coward, so he doesn't come near the house. He shows up on campus and takes Bobbi to lunch sometimes. I guess, even though he's retired from the local force, he has a few friends. However it happens, he seems to get her class schedule, so he can show up whenever he wants without appearing to be stalking her."

"How does Bobbi feel about that," Edna wondered aloud.

Louise lifted a shoulder. "Says she doesn't mind, but I think she's not making a fuss because she knows it will upset Duke and me. She's a sensitive and warm-hearted young woman, so I think as long as John behaves, she'll put up with him."

"Does your husband mind John coming back into your lives?"

"John isn't back in my life," Louise protested. "I want nothing to do with the man, but to answer your question, Duke wasn't a bit happy. As long as John keeps his distance, there's not much we can do, though. It's just something we live with, watching over our shoulder."

When Edna left the Callahan home shortly thereafter, she had a lot to think about, but all that went out of her head as she checked her cell phone. She'd left it in the car so as not to be disturbed while she was talking to Bobbi. Now, she noticed several calls from Matthew, but only one short message. "Call as soon as you can."

She did.

The first words out of his mouth were, "Don't worry. Dad's okay." Taken by surprise, Edna was speechless, so Matthew repeated. "He's okay. We got him back onboard in less than fifteen minutes."

"What are you talking about? What happened?" By now, Edna's heart was racing. She had a sudden urge to laugh, but swallowed hard and took a deep breath. "Please, Matthew. Tell me what happened." Then, she changed her mind. "Is your father there? Put him on the phone."

"No. Yes." Matthew stuttered and then seemed to take a deep breath himself. "He's here, in the hospital. Patrick's doctor checked him over and Dad will be fine. I think mainly he's just shaken up a bit."

"If he's fine, why is he in the hospital?" Edna wasn't feeling reassured. "What happened?" Her patience was beginning to wear thin with this son of Albert's. He was *her* son only when he wasn't exasperating her.

"He bumped his head when he fell overboard. We don't know *how* exactly. One minute we were fishing and the next thing we knew, Dad was shouting at us from the water. He was floundering because of his bad leg. I jumped in, and Ken threw me a ring. Course, we all had on life jackets, so nobody was really in big trouble." Matthew went on to explain how he swam Albert to the side of the boat with a lifeguard hold. Roger and his brother had to lean down to grab Albert's arms and pull him up the side of the boat. Apparently, it was too hard for him to climb up the ladder, again because of his injured leg, and he was a little groggy because of the knock on his head.

Matthew ended by saying, "I asked Dad if he wanted to leave earlier than planned. He said no, he doesn't want to spoil the trip, but he asked me to call and let you know he's okay."

So I'll be sure to coddle him when he gets here, Edna thought with a grin, but didn't say aloud. Instead, she asked, "What do the doctors say? Could your father have fainted or had a touch of heat stroke?"

"They're not sure. Maybe all the above. Hard to say, but they've checked him out and say he should be fine to fly tomorrow."

"*Should* be," Edna echoed weakly.

Chapter 23

When she reached home, having dwelt for the entire trip on her husband's accident and how he might have simply fallen off a boat, Edna phoned her daughter-in-law.

"Have you talked to Matt?" Irene asked as soon as preliminary greetings were over.

"Yes, and I'm worried about Albert, but there's nothing to be done until they get home. I'll see if he'll go get checked over by his own physician, but I don't hold out much hope. You know how stubborn he can be." She spoke more lightly than she felt and changed the subject. "How's Lettie?"

"Oh, my goodness, I think I'm beginning to regret getting involved with the Becks."

Edna was surprised at the irritation in Irene's tone. It took a lot to rattle this mother of four, but she did sound annoyed. "What's happened?"

"Rosie has apparently decided to take Lettie to her grandmother's, first thing in the morning. Talk about a ping pong ball. I don't know what's going on with that woman. Tomorrow is Valentine's Day, the day she's been working toward for weeks. Now, it sounds like she's skipping out on her employer, only to take her daughter back to her grandmother's. Just the reverse of what she did a few days ago. Why would she remove the child, leave Lettie with me during the day and then suddenly turn around and take her back to Lily?" Irene paused to take a deep breath before adding. "If that child doesn't become neurotic in the next few years, it won't be her mother's fault."

"Do you think Rosie's been fired?" Edna was as surprised and concerned as her daughter-in-law sounded.

"Maybe after the big day, but certainly not before. This seems like very erratic behavior, Edna. I'm worried about Lettie and the effects on her. What should I do? What *can* I do?"

Edna was wondering the same thing. "I'll visit Lily tomorrow. I want to talk to her again anyway, so maybe I can learn what's going on." She ended the call soon thereafter and headed for the grocery store.

For the rest of the day, Edna busied herself cooking and straightened the house, so she wouldn't sit and ruminate on Albert's health or Rosie's strange actions or Louise Callahan's revelations. While a chicken was simmering, preparatory to making soup, she puttered around the house putting away her knitting, music discs and books. Beverly and Junie of Housekeeper Helpers would arrive in the morning to clean, so Edna got rid of any clutter that might be in their way. She then made cranberry cake, a favorite of Albert's. She thought the homemade soup would not only be comforting, but would also ward off any cold or flu bugs that might be hanging around in his body after a dunk in the ocean. She planned to pamper her husband when he got home, and maybe he'd feel mellow enough to allow her to make a doctor's appointment for him.

Benjamin followed her around the house, inspecting

her work and, occasionally, undoing her straightening with a swipe of his paw to a tatted doily on the arm of a chair or a stack of papers on the desk in the office. Edna indulged him with a chuckle as he finally settled on a cushioned chair in the kitchen to watch as she deboned the chicken.

The antics of her cat and the chores kept Edna's mind occupied for several hours. With the work done, in the late afternoon, Edna poured herself a glass of wine, lit a small fire in the hearth and settled in her favorite chair with her notebook. It was time to concentrate. She had written down several questions earlier in the week, when she'd been sitting in the mall parking lot, hiding from John Forrester. Now, she wanted to review and update her notes. She wanted to be prepared to press Lily tomorrow. Edna was convinced the woman knew much more than she'd admitted.

By now, Edna was as certain as she could be that Gregory Haverstrum had been poisoned, and most likely, the substance he'd ingested was ranunculin. Clem Peppafitch had the bloom of a Christmas Rose clutched in his hand at the time of his death. Coincidence? She was beginning to doubt it very strongly. She may be accused of watching too many crime shows on TV, but Edna was convinced he was trying to tell them something.

Charlie reported that Clem had died of an overdose of digitalis, but Peppa said he wouldn't have taken the drug. Why not? Could he, too, have been poisoned?

Edna made a mental note to corner Peppa that evening at Mary's and find out why she disagreed with the medical examiner's conclusion. Through online research, Edna had learned that the symptoms of too much digitalis in the body can cause confusion and impair vision. That would be precisely why Clem looked to be stumbling and disoriented, as if he were drunk.

Thinking about some of the other plants she'd seen in Lily Beck's garden, Edna went into her office and scanned through Mrs. Rabichek's journals. She stopped speed-reading and carefully re-read the information on Pieris japonica, more commonly known as "lily of the valley shrub." She looked particularly at the red notations, Mrs. Rabichek's color coding for warnings. *"Mad honey" made from the plants can cause cardiac arrhythmias, mild paralysis, convulsions. Also, muscular weakness, impaired vision. Serious cardiovascular effects: bradycardia, hypotension (caused by vasodilation), atrioventricular block. May be lethal.*

Carefully returning the journal to its place on the shelf, Edna went back to her seat by the fire. She speculated. If Clem felt his heart going into overdrive, he might have taken digitalis to slow it down. Maybe he panicked and took too much. She already knew that the symptoms of the overdose would make it appear as if he were drunk. Had he been trying to get away from the Beck house and seek safety with Peppa? If so, why?

And what about the "mad honey" Edna had just read about. According to Mrs. Rabichek's warnings, that would also slow one's heartbeat. Lily had said she'd stopped keeping bees because of the potentially tainted honey. Had she kept some from that one year's harvest?

Quite a lot of what Edna was finding circled around

to Lily, but what about Rosie? Certainly she had as much access to the garden as did her mother, and she must also be knowledgeable about all sorts of vegetation after working in a nursery.

I wonder. Retrieving her small notebook, Edna played with her pencil for a few minutes, idly and almost subconsciously sketching the blossoms of the Christmas Rose. Why had Clem been carrying a rose? Had he been planting so simple a clue?

Edna suddenly wanted to discuss the idea with Charlie. She pushed herself out of her chair and almost ran to her office. He must meet her at the Beck house tomorrow.

Receiving no answer from the detective's cell phone, Edna figured he must be working and unable to pick up her call. She left a message and, wanting to be certain he knew how important her request was, she phoned the station and left the same message with the man on duty.

"Yes, ma'am." He'd be sure to deliver the message to Detective Rogers. "Urgent. Yes, ma'am."

With a sigh, Edna hung up the phone. That was all she could do tonight. In another couple of hours, she needed to be at Mary's. After a light supper and a short nap, Edna was ready to face the evening ahead.

"No, Benjamin. I want you to stay here in the house," she said to the ginger cat before she stepped outside the back door and waited for her eyes to adjust to the darkness. Clouds obscured the moon, so there was hardly any natural light to guide her, but the temperature seemed almost mild. She switched on the flashlight she'd taken from a shelf in the mudroom. From the dimness of the bulb, she could tell the batteries were low, but she didn't want to take the time to go back for new ones. Certainly, they would last until she crossed to the neighboring house.

Plodding carefully over the uneven lawn, Edna saw light coming from Mary's kitchen. Tuck and Peppa must have arrived. As Edna reached the barway in the stone wall between the properties, her flashlight went out. Stopping to shake the heavy metal tube, she was rewarded with a faint glow. The moment she lifted her head to continue her walk, she saw a light go on in Mary's attic.

"They've started without me," she muttered, but before she could take another step, the upper story went dark. *Odd*, she thought, staring at the top floor of the house. She started forwarded again, mindful of her footing, but looked up sharply when light again appeared in the attic window. *It's as if someone were turning on a three-way light*, she thought, watching the brightness grow in stages before being extinguished again.

Picking up speed, she hurried as fast as she dared across the rest of the lawn, hardly noticing that her own light had gone out as she reached the packed-dirt driveway and along to Mary's back door. When she passed the kitchen window, she saw all three women in the room.

So who would be upstairs in the nursery? Edna wondered.

She entered the back hall, left her coat on a peg near the door and went through into the kitchen, surprised not to be greeted by Hank or Ink Spot. The thought of

Mary's pets vanished from her mind as she moved into the kitchen and spotted her neighbor. "Who's in your attic?"

She'd apparently startled Tuck and Peppa who spun around at the sound of her voice. Mary had been leaning back against the counter, facing the door. She frowned. "What do you mean?" Then, realization seemed to strike as her expression changed from confusion to excitement. "What did you see? Did you see my ghost?"

"There's a light going on and off in your attic. Do you have a lamp on a timer? If so, there must be a short in it." Edna had reached what she thought was a sensible answer, if there was nobody else in the house.

"Don't have anything up there on a timer," Mary insisted. Still looking happily excited, she said, "Let's go see."

Tuck's eyes had grown wide and she was beginning to look nervous, but Peppa seemed as eager as Mary. *"Lay on, Macduff, and damned be him who first cries Hold! Enough!"*

"Do you think you should be quoting Macbeth?" Tuck asked in a low, shaky voice. "Isn't that bad luck?"

"We're not in a theater," Peppa retorted.

"Hush. Don't want to scare 'im," Mary hissed, even though nobody had yet left the room.

Edna felt the urge to laugh aloud at the drama played out by the other three, but bit her tongue so as not to offend her friends. *But really, this is too comical*, she thought. Following the troupe toward the living room and the front stairs, however, she had to admit to a prickling sensation growing between her shoulder blades.

The back stairs were closer to the kitchen, but the front ones provided a more direct climb to the nursery side of the third floor. Mary led the way and Edna noticed that each of the women carried flashlights. Imitating the slow tiptoeing of her friends up the wide staircase, she suddenly wished she'd taken the time to replace her batteries. Still, she held the heavy metal tube in her hand, in case she needed to defend herself.

Mary halted on the third-floor landing and waited outside the nursery until the women all stood together.

"Open it," whispered Peppa.

As Mary reached for the knob, a ribbon of light appeared in the crack beneath the door. She jerked her hand back as if she'd been burned, and the women all stared as the radiance brightened and then disappeared. In that brief instance, Edna saw everyone's eyes were as large as hers felt. She was wondering if their spines were as tingly as hers, too, when the sound of pattering feet sounded from the other side of the flimsy wooden door. Whatever made the sound was running away.

Peppa nudged Mary's upper arm with her flashlight. "Go on. Open it," she repeated her earlier command. "We're right behind you."

Again, Edna felt the urge to laugh, but bit down hard on her lip. It was more of a nervous reaction than comic now.

Reaching out hesitantly, Mary took hold of the knob, twisted and thrust the door wide. She pushed so hard, the door banged against the wall and bounced back, slamming shut. In the second or two that the door had been open, Edna hadn't seen anything ghostlike.

"Oh, phooey," Peppa said. Elbowing Mary aside,

she grabbed the handle, opened the door and walked into the room. The others followed with Edna bringing up the rear.

As soon as she moved to stand beside Tuck, Edna saw the flash of eyes an instant before they disappeared. Mary must have seen them, too, because she directed the beam of her light across to the far wall from where faint scratching noises emanated. She was just quick enough to catch two tails disappear behind a wooden chest, one white and the other black. At once, Mary reached to the side and tapped a floor lamp, turning it on.

"A touch light?" Edna guessed.

At Mary's nod and sheepish look, Edna began to laugh. She couldn't hold it back any longer and neither, did it seem, could the other women. Even Mary joined in.

When they finally had control of themselves, the quartet moved as one to the trunk.

"My toy box," Mary explained.

The scratched and battered container, looking much like a storybook pirate's chest, stood next to the two steps that led up to the storage room door and about five inches out from the wall.

Leaving enough room for the rounded lid to be lifted, Edna mused. Putting her hand on a back corner, she pushed the chest askew to see where the cats had gone.

"Forgot about that space under the stairs," Mary said, bending over the trunk. "Help me move this," she said to Edna. "I want to get those cats out of there. Can't imagine how they got up here in the first place. I left 'em in Father's room."

Peppa also helped to shove the trunk farther from the wall, allowing the women to examine the hollow area beneath the stairs, but no cats were to be found. Instead, when Mary crouched down to shine her light in the hole, she spotted an opening in the rear panel.

Sounding slightly panicked, she sputtered, "They're in the wall. They're gonna get stuck."

"Nonsense," Edna said, putting a hand on Mary's shoulder to calm her. "If the noises you've been hearing have been those cats all along, they must have found a passage from your father's room. You said there was a secret staircase somewhere in the house. I think we've just found it."

"Exciting," Peppa said. "It's what I love about these old places. Full of nooks, crannies and secrets." She gave a hoot of laughter. "Let's go see where they've gotten to. Your father's old room, did you say?"

When the women reached the floor below and entered Mr. Osbourne's former bedroom, Auntie Bea was sitting in the middle of a braided run, watching sedately while two half-grown kittens, one black and the other white, tumbled and wrestled before her.

Peppa ignored the antics as she looked around the room, focused her eyes on the right-hand wall against which stood a canopied antique bed. "Must be here," she muttered, getting down on hands and knees and throwing back the spread to shine her flashlight underneath. Seconds later, she lifted her head, eyes glowing with triumph. "Yep. It's here all right. Paneling's been pushed aside. Bet you never noticed it was slanted cause of the fabric behind the headboard. When's the last time you took that down to have it cleaned?"

Mary scowled, obviously offended. "Get's done every year."

Edna spoke up in Mary's defense. "If I know kittens, they probably found a weak spot in the wood and played with it until it broke loose."

Mary brightened at the idea. "Yes, and I bet Auntie Bea helped so she could follow her charges when they disappeared." Turning to look fondly down at the Maine Coon, Mary explained to the others in the room, "She's fiercely protective of Snowball and Charcoal." Speaking to the other women, she said, "I'd better close that up before they get stuck or hurt themselves. Who knows what else they might find in there to get themselves into trouble."

That said, she went downstairs and returned with a hammer and nails. As she crawled beneath the bed to secure the panel back into place, two spirited kittens decided to help. When she was able to stop laughing enough to plead for some assistance with her four-legged friends, Tuck got down on hands and knees on the opposite side of the bed. Peppa placed a hand on the mattress, preparing to join Tuck when Edna stopped her.

"A moment, if you will, Peppa." Edna took hold of her friend's arm and drew her gently away from the activity. "I need to ask about Clem. Why are you so certain that he didn't die of a digitalis overdose?"

Peppa was keeping her eyes on the other women, and Edna suspected she would rather be beneath the bed, checking on Mary's work, if not supervising it. The old librarian spoke a bit sharply, as if the facts were common knowledge. "He's got ... rather he *had* a thyroid problem that caused his heart to beat slower than normal." She turned to look at Edna, her forehead wrinkled with confusion. "Is that really what they're saying? He had digitalis in his system?"

Edna nodded. She was speechless as she considered what Peppa had just told her. "So any sort of medication for a fibrillating heart …"

"Right," Peppa interrupted. "With Clem's condition, it would slow his heart down to the point that he would faint … or worse."

"Cause his heart to stop," Edna concluded.

"Darn fool." Peppa shook her head and turned away, but not before Edna saw the moisture in the old librarian's eyes.

Without another word, she moved back toward the bed and the sound of more laughter and hammering and meowing coming from underneath. Edna remained where she was, lost in the thought, *I should go to Lily's and check Clem's belongings.*

Chapter 24

Once the bedroom and adjoining bathroom had been inspected for any other loose boards or potential hazards, Mary shut the cats up for the night. After checking on Hank and Spot to assure them that all was well, she led the women downstairs. In order to unwind from the night's excitement, the four women sat at the dining room table for another hour, drinking tea and talking about old houses, secret passages and cats.

"It's always been amazing to me," said Edna, "that a ten pound, scampering cat can sound like a heavy-footed child." She knew Mary was still feeling foolish over making such a big fuss over a ghost in her attic. Not only that, but the crime enthusiast had admitted to being afraid to investigate alone.

When Edna finally went home and to bed shortly before midnight, she slept fitfully. She was worried that Matthew wasn't telling her the entire story and wondered how Albert was really doing. Was he in pain? Had he set his knee rehabilitation back when he fell off the boat? Had he picked up some sort of harmful bacteria by swallowing sea water?

When she finally stopped agonizing over Albert, her thoughts turned to Mary's cats finding the hidden staircase to the attic. Peppa's theory was that the passage was the master's means of visiting the maids' quarters.

Tuck thought it more likely the runaway slaves used the stairs to mount to the top of the house in order to hide in the false front around the chimney, or perhaps they hid between the walls, on the steps themselves.

Protection, Edna thought, turning over and bunching the pillow beneath her head. *Fiercely protective.* Mary had said that about Auntie Bea and the kittens. Edna came fully awake from a half sleep, half dream state. Who else had said that to her recently? She relaxed again when she remembered it had been Louise Callahan. Duke was fiercely protective of Bobbi. Wouldn't let John Forrester harm her.

Who else? Edna struggled in her mind, tensing again as she turned onto her right side and pulled the covers up to her chin. Thinking back, she pictured herself in Lily Beck's sun room, listening to the woman. Rosie. *Rose has always been fiercely protective of Violet, from the moment that baby was placed in her arms at the hospital.*

Violet ... what was it that Lettie had said? Lily's medicine didn't make him better, meaning Gregory. Had Lettie given something to her father in hopes of curing him, but killing him instead?

Rosie ... Rose, Edna's head throbbed with the word. *Clem was holding a rose. Was it meant to be a clue? Must talk to Charlie ... must talk to Charlie.* Edna finally fell into a dreamless sleep at four o'clock.

She awoke three hours later, feeling groggy, so she decided to get up. Downstairs, she phoned Charlie. When a sleepy voice answered on the third ring, she said, "Sorry I woke you, Charlie, but since you're up, come for breakfast. There are things we need to discuss.

Scrambled eggs and popovers in half an hour."

It took the detective closer to an hour before he knocked on the back door and let himself in, carrying three pink roses that he handed to Edna. "Happy Valentine's Day."

"Why, how thoughtful." Edna accepted the flowers, giving her favorite policeman a peck on the cheek. She knew that pink denoted admiration and wondered if he did, too. She was certain Starling would receive multiple red roses from him sometime today and smiled, thinking of how kind this police detective could be. "Help yourself to coffee and sit," she commanded, retrieving a small vase from a low cupboard and arranging the roses for the table. "I thought you'd be late, so held off cooking the eggs. Won't take but a minute, though."

As they ate breakfast, the small amount of chatter was confined to food and the weather. Charlie finally wiped his mouth, laid his napkin aside, and rose to refill both his coffee cup and Edna's. Resuming his seat, he said, "Okay. What's so important you got me out of bed at this ungodly hour?" His grin belied the gruffness of the question.

"Peppa told me last night that Clem wouldn't have taken digitalis."

Charlie nodded. "Peggy King told me. Matter of fact, the thyroid condition was on the autopsy report."

Edna waved a hand dismissively. "So, if he didn't overdose, either accidentally or on purpose, then someone else must have given him the drug." She looked across at the detective with her most serious expression. "I've been thinking about this most of last night. If Clem wasn't taking a rose to Peppa, why did he have it in his hand and why clutched so tightly? Furthermore, what was he doing in her neighborhood? How did he get there?"

"Million dollar question," Charlie said, sipping his coffee as he studied her face.

When he said nothing further, Edna continued. "What if he discovered who poisoned Gregory Haverstrum? I can only think it had to be Lily or Rose or ... heaven forbid, Violet. He might have discovered the poison and confronted the killer. It's the only thing that makes sense of his death."

Charlie raised an eyebrow. "Violet?"

Edna repeated what Lettie had said about Lily's medicine. "It really doesn't bear thinking, but I have to admit, it *is* possible."

Charlie leaned forward and, putting aside his coffee, clasped his hands together on the table. "Okay. Let's, for a moment, suppose someone in the Beck's household killed Haverstrum and Peppafitch found out. Where's the proof?"

"That's what I was hoping you'd help me with," Edna said, feeling a twinge of excitement over the prospect of some positive action. "I want to get into Clem's apartment. There must be something in his place that might provide a clue. Maybe he left a note," she added, feeling the steam go out of her enthusiasm.

"Peggy looked around his apartment Sunday morning. Didn't spot anything out of the ordinary, from what she told me."

"But she didn't know about the digitalis then. We have more information on what to look for now." She told him what she'd read about "mad honey."

Charlie didn't respond as eager as she'd hoped. He looked at his watch. "I have a meeting with the chief that will probably last most of the morning. I'm not promising anything, but I will meet you at the Beck house this afternoon. Say about one-thirty?"

Edna knew her face had fallen. She wanted to leave immediately, not waste any more time.

He reached across the table and gently squeezed her wrist. "We don't have a warrant, nor do we have much of a reason for snooping in Clem's rooms. All we can do is ask Lily if we can go look around. If she says no, I'm afraid that will be it."

Edna tried to feel optimistic. "She won't say no. Why would she?"

As it turned out, Edna didn't have to wait until the afternoon to visit Lily Beck. An hour after Charlie left, the woman herself phoned and invited Edna to lunch. "My daughter and granddaughter are with me through the weekend. You were so gracious to Violet, I'd like to return some of your hospitality. Violet, also, asked particularly if you could join us."

Edna was both nervous and excited as noon approached. She went through her wardrobe twice, trying to decide whether or not to wear a dress, but eventually settled on charcoal-gray woolen slacks with a forest-green silk blouse. The choice was made when she thought of rummaging through Clem Peppafitch's living quarters. She'd be more comfortable in trousers.

She was so preoccupied that she nearly forgot to phone Charlie. Thinking that his meeting must be over after nearly three hours, she was disappointed when he didn't answer his cell. She wanted to tell him personally

about Lily's luncheon invitation and let him know that
he needn't meet her later. When the "speak beep"
sounded, Edna sighed and left a message.

"You won't guess, Charlie," she began. "Lily
phoned after you left this morning and has invited me to
join her, Rosie and Lettie for lunch. I'm certain I can
come up with a plausible reason for her to let me into
Clem's apartment. No need for you to meet me at her
place. It should be fairly straight-forward for me to
search his place, and since we'll be driving together to
the airport this evening, I'll fill you in then with
whatever I find. I hope your meeting went well." With
that, Edna hung up, got into her coat and left the house
at eleven forty-five.

Chapter 25

"It's about time you got here. Did you forget your key?" Lily Beck's voice came out as the door was swinging open.

Traffic being light, Edna had pulled up onto the bungalow's driveway several minutes earlier than expected, but decided to ring the bell instead of sitting in her car. Most hosts she knew were ready before the guests were actually due to arrive. Of course, there were exceptions.

"Am I late?" she said, taken aback by Lily's brusqueness.

Lily's expression softened, but only slightly. "Of course not. I thought you were my daughter." She drew the door wider to let Edna into the hall. "Unless you're very hungry, I'll hold lunch for a while. Rose took Violet shopping and they haven't returned yet. I don't know what's gotten into her. I told her specifically to be home before noon."

Edna saw her chance to visit the garage and to distract Lily's irritation at the same time. "It's really no problem. I can wait to eat." Uncertain and a bit nervous as to how Lily would take the request, Edna plunged ahead. "As a matter of fact, I would like to ask a small favor of you, and perhaps now would be a good time."

"Oh?" Lily frowned, looking wary.

"Yes. You see, I was hoping to get a look at Clem's apartment. Peppa is a friend of mine, and I know how distressed she is over his death. It would be too upsetting for her to inspect his place herself. I imagine she'd feel she had no right, since she and Clem have been divorced for so many years. I thought if you would allow me, I could look over his belongings to see if there might be something personal of his that she would like to have. You know, an old photograph or a watch. Something along those lines." Edna knew she was babbling, but Lily was simply standing in the hallway, staring at her. When the woman still said nothing after Edna paused for breath, she decided to play her last card. "Perhaps in the process, I could box up his effects, so the apartment can be cleaned for your next handyman or tenant."

At the suggestion, Lily finally reacted. "Of course. Wait here. I'll get my coat and the keys."

Minutes later, Edna stood beside her host at the side door to the garage which stood slightly ajar.

Lily shook her head as she pushed the door wider. "Rose and Violet are too careless about closing doors. They know I don't like things left open."

Not an auspicious beginning, Edna thought as she followed her host into the building.

The black Impala was parked in the first bay. Clem's battered old pickup stood in the fourth and farthest. Partially hidden by the truck's bed, a set of stairs rose to a small landing, then turned and ran up the far side of the building to the apartment above. Between the empty second and third bays were a snow blower, a gas-powered rototiller and an electric lawn mower. The machines, lined up neatly, one behind the other, looked old but well maintained.

The room itself was immaculate. Pegboard had been mounted on either end of the back wall. The one in front of the Impala held hammers, screwdrivers, wrenches, plyers and assorted other small hand tools. On the wall facing Clem's vehicle hung saws of various sizes, along with automotive and gardening tools. Below the pegboard at the far bay was a workbench, beneath which stood a backless bar stool. Under the stairs leading to the overhead rooms, Edna spotted the tops of several toolboxes lined up along the wall beyond the hood of the truck.

"And they left those lights on." Lily was obviously not pleased. "Costs money. I suppose my granddaughter has been playing in here again." Her annoyed tone drew Edna's attention away from the examination of her surroundings, and she looked up to see that the long florescent ceiling lights over the third space and over Clem's vehicle were indeed aglow. "And that door." Another burst from Lily. "Those cupboards should be locked. Someone's been in my pantry closets."

She hastened around the car's hood and headed for a row of tall, shallow cupboards built into the middle section of the rear garage wall. When Edna approached behind her hostess and looked over Lily's shoulder, she saw shelves had been built from floor level to about six feet. Quarts of beans, tomatoes and pickles were arranged two deep. Pints of jams and honey were double-stacked, as well. On top of each cupboard were old cookie and candy tins, most painted with Christmas scenes. Edna supposed they were empty, but only because her own would be. She perked up instantly when Lily removed a jar of honey from a shelf at eye level and turned to hold it up to the light. It was less than half full.

"Looks like Clem helped himself to my supplies." She sounded more surprised than upset. Edna shivered at the woman's cold tone when she said, "Guess he got what he deserved then."

"What do you mean?"

"I mean," Lily said, turning to face Edna and extending the jar for a better view, "that this is the honey I told you about. I kept some, even after the beekeeper's warning that it could make me sick. Since the hive sat next to my Lily of the Valley shrub, he figured the bees fed on it to the exclusion of other blossoms." She frowned for a second or two before adding, "Didn't think it would be lethal, though."

"If that's true that the bees fed off the Pieris japonica, what you're holding would be what's known as 'mad honey'," Edna said, as a piece of her puzzle fell into place. "I've been reading about it in Mrs. Rabichek's journal."

"And what have you read? Will it indeed make someone sick? Please don't tell me it would be fatal to whoever ate it."

"It shouldn't." Edna thought the time was not right to inform Lily about the thyroid condition that caused Clem's heart to beat slower than normal and that this honey would have repressed the rate even more. Since they were on the subject, however, she said, "I have learned quite a lot about herbal remedies in Mrs. Rabichek's journals, to the extent that I'm thinking of putting some of the plants in my yard to use." Hoping she sounded naïve enough, she went on. "Something Lettie … er, something *Violet* said makes me think that you might be knowledgeable about natural remedies."

Lily's eyes narrowed as she studied Edna. "Oh? What did she say to make you think that?"

"Well," Edna hesitated, wondering how thin the ice was on which she was treading. "She happened to see a sketch I made of a Christmas Rose blossom and mentioned that she saw you making medicine from the flower."

Lily's face flushed. "I don't know where she got that idea. Violet's watched me propagate plants many times, but I don't remember ever telling her that I was making medicine."

Edna felt her temper begin to rise and tried to keep irritation from her voice. Was Lily hiding guilty secrets? "She told me that your medicine didn't make her father feel better. What did she mean?"

Instead of answering, Lily turned to replace the jar on the shelf, so Edna wasn't able see her expression. "I'm sure I don't know."

Edna thought she'd better be careful in phrasing her next questions. She didn't feel good about using the child this way, but she had to get Lily to talk. If upsetting her would do the trick, then Edna had to try.

"Does Violet have access to these cupboards? You said you thought she might have been playing in here." Edna raised a palm to indicate the overhead lights, reminding Lily of her earlier remark. "If she misunderstood and thought you did make remedies, she could have taken something from these shelves to help cure Gregory's flu two years ago. Do you think that's possible?"

"Nobody has access to these cupboards but me." Still with her back to Edna, Lily chose a small key on the ring in her hand and locked the door. By the time she turned around to face Edna, Lily seemed to have regained some composure. Brusquely, she said, "I must have forgotten to close and lock the door properly. It probably swung open on its own."

"Children are very inquisitive and seem to know things we are certain they don't," Edna said. She carefully avoided any mention of the missing honey which would make it fairly plain that the cupboards weren't as secure as Lily implied. "Do you think your granddaughter might have discovered where you keep your keys?"

"I hide them in my kitchen," Lily said, sounding smug. "Even if she found them, they'd be only a bunch of keys to her. She wouldn't have any way to know they open doors here in the garage."

Edna wasn't convinced. The girl could have seen her grandmother use the keys. Children do have a memory for small details, as Edna only knew from raising four of her own. Now was not the time to argue the point with her host, however. More important matters needed dealing with. "It is conceivable that Violet misconstrued something you said, but you should be aware that she is intrigued with what she considers your 'medicine.' Her comment leads me to believe she gave something you made to her father, thinking it would make him feel better." Edna paused there. She didn't want to voice the obvious. If Lettie gave ranunculin to her father, she'd be his unwitting killer. The honey was here in the cupboard and might have been what poisoned Clem, but where was the Christmas Rose potion? Was there some still here in the garage? Pushing the distracting thought to the back of her mind, Edna said, "I'm afraid I have to mention Violet's comment to the police. They're going to want to question her."

"You're not going to say anything to the police."

Both women spun around at the sound of Rosie's voice. Edna wondered how long the young woman had been standing on the other side of the Impala and how much she had heard. At that moment, Rose rounded the hood, swiping at the pegboard as she passed between the car and the back wall. "Nobody's questioning my daughter."

"Rose?" Lily spoke her daughter's name as a question. After a brief hesitation, she said, "It's about time you got home. Lunch will be cold, but we'd better go eat. Where's Violet?"

Edna suspected Lily was trying to divert Rosie's obvious anger. Edna's eyes didn't leave the younger woman's face as she stopped beside her mother and glared at Edna.

"Rose, put that thing down," Lily snapped. She was holding her key ring tightly against her chest with both hands. Edna thought she could see fright in the woman's eyes as she stared at her daughter.

Lily's comment made Edna look at the hand Rosie had half-hidden behind her thigh. In it was clutched an ice pick. The five-inch, narrow shaft looked rusty and there appeared to be a crack in the old wooden handle, but Edna knew the point would be sharp … and dangerous … and deadly. Her eyes sprung back to Rosie's and she took an involuntary step back from the malice she saw in them. Having heard of the woman's erratic behavior from Irene, Edna suspected Rosie was losing control of her emotions, but never expected to see the madness in her eyes as was now evident.

"Nobody's taking my daughter from me." Rosie hissed the words.

Edna wondered if it were even possible to reason with the woman, but she had to try. "You asked me to help, Rosie," she said in what she hoped was a reassuring tone. "Remember? The truth needs to come out, if the suspicion and bullying are to stop. We talked about that. You and your daughter should be able to live in peace, but that won't happen until people know what happened two years ago."

Rosie shook her head, still angry. "Lettie was never supposed to be the one to suffer. Our troubles should have been over once Gregory was dead." She gave a short menacing laugh. "He thought he could take her from me and leave me with nothing."

"Rose, what are you saying?" Lily's voice was firm. "I think you should stop talking now. We should go back to the house. Lunch is …"

"Don't you know?" Rosie interrupted, sliding her eyes quickly toward her mother and back to Edna. Clearly, she believed that Edna posed a threat and needed to be watched carefully. "He was going to take Lettie away. I couldn't let him do that," she said. She lifted her arm and pointed the ice pick at Edna. "Nobody is going to question her, either." She took a step toward

Edna.

"Hold it right there, Miz Beck."

Edna had little time to enjoy the sound of Charlie's voice as Rosie leaped. Her left arm wrapped around Edna's neck as she circled and spun to look back at Charlie in the open doorway. It had taken Rosie less than two seconds to pull Edna against her chest and press the ice pick against Edna's throat.

Charlie moved his arms out to the side with his hands spread, palms down, in a placating gesture. "You don't want to do anything foolish, Miz Beck," he said, walking slowly around the Impala's hood. "Just put the pick down and let Edna go." As he spoke, he continued to move slowly in their direction.

"Do as he says, Rose." Lily spoke harshly, as if to a recalcitrant child, but stayed where she was, her hands still held protectively against her chest.

Rosie began to back away from Charlie, pulling Edna with her. "Don't come any closer." Her voice wavered slightly and some confusion seemed to creep into her tone when she said, "We're going to get in the truck. Nobody is to follow or she will die." As she spoke, Rosie kept backing up while Charlie kept walking steadily toward them.

Edna wanted to get a foot behind Rosie's ankle to try and trip her, but she was having difficulty simply staying on her feet as she was dragged backwards. Holding tightly to the arm around her neck to keep from falling, she realized Rosie was very strong. Edna changed her grip on the woman's arm, preparing to sink her fingernails, however short, into the flesh.

"Stay where you are or I swear I'll kill her." Rosie

sounded more controlled and very angry, as if she'd come to a decision. "Lily, go get Lettie. She's locked in her room, but the key is in the door."

"No." Now Lily sounded more determined than frightened, and Edna was certain the woman would protect her grandchild from falling victim to Rosie's irrational behavior.

"You don't want to do that, Miz Beck," Charlie spoke quickly, then more slowly to remove the edge of panic from his voice. "Let Edna go and we can talk. If you want to leave, I'll go with you." Charlie managed to keep his tone low and soothing.

Rosie coughed a mirthless laugh into Edna's left ear. "I'm not stupid enough to take a cop with me. This lady's coming with me and so is my daughter." Her voice grew louder and, Edna thought, more desperate. "What are you waiting for, Lily." It wasn't a question. "I said go get Lettie. *Now*."

Edna saw Charlie's eyes flick above and beyond the pick in Rosie's hand and wondered what he was thinking. Did he have a plan to get her out of this? Was he judging the distance to Clem's truck? She kept her eyes on his, prepared for any signal he might give her. Rosie took another wobbly step backward, pulling Edna with her. The movement caused the pick's cold metal tip to jab Edna's skin, but she refused to be distracted.

At that moment, Charlie flicked his eyes to Edna's left and feinted toward Rosie's right hand.

Ready for his move, Edna twisted her head and rolled her shoulders away from the weapon, more in reflex than conscious thought. She was certain Rosie would now push the pick farther into her neck and determined to go out fighting. As she felt Rosie's arm slip from her neck, Edna kicked back, feeling the hard rubber heel of her shoe connect with the woman's shin. Surprised that her struggling had loosened Rosie's hold on her, Edna pulled down on Rosie's arm. At once, Rosie yelled and clawed Edna's shoulder. She seemed to be the one who was falling, not Edna.

In the same two seconds it took Edna to move, Charlie grabbed her wrist and drew her toward him. As soon as she felt her captor's grip ease, Edna spun to face Rosie. What she saw made her gasp. John Forrester was grappling with Rosie. His left arm was around her waist, lifting her far enough from the floor that she had to balance on tiptoes. His right hand had hold of Rosie's wrist and, by the look on her face, he was squeezing hard.

"Drop it," he snarled, giving her hand a quick shake.

After a brief struggle, all energy suddenly seemed to leave Rosie's body as she dropped the ice pick. She would have collapsed to the floor if it weren't for John's arm holding her like a rag doll.

Lily seemed to come alive when her daughter crumpled. "Here," she shouted, rushing forward. "Let her go."

John obeyed and Lily folded her daughter into her arms. Both women slid to the cement floor, mother holding a sobbing child to her breast.

Grabbing the pick off the floor, John stepped around them and extended the weapon, handle first, to Charlie. He then shook Charlie's hand, all the while ignoring Edna. "Glad you came along, son," he said.

"Glad you were behind that truck," Charlie said, accepting the man's hand with a grin.

"Have you been there all along?" Edna stared at the retired detective in disbelief.

John had the decency to look sheepish. "Yep."

"How'd you happen to be here?" Charlie asked.

John shrugged a shoulder. "Drove by this morning and noticed the open door. Thought I'd make sure nobody was stealing Miz Beck's tools. You know how burglars are," he said, wiping a hand over his face before glancing at Charlie from beneath lowered lids. "Anyone reading the handyman's obit in the paper might think the place was unprotected. Didn't see any sense in upsetting the house if everything was secure, so I showed myself in. Good thing, huh?"

John maneuvered the subject away from his illegal trespassing, but perhaps was unaware he was implicating himself in an illegal search as he turned his head and jutted his chin toward the center back wall of the garage. "I was looking to see what was in those cupboards when I heard someone coming this way. Thought I'd just rest myself over on those stairs behind the truck and keep out of their way." Again, he merely slid his eyes in Charlie's direction, probably to see how his tale was being received. "You know, in case they were planning to rob the place."

"Well, glad you decided to stay and make sure all was safe," Charlie agreed, reaching into his breast pocket for his cell phone. "Right now, I think I'd better call this in."

"I don't see a reason for me to hang around. I'll drop by the station later, if you want a statement." John

Forrester headed for the door, without another word or glance at Edna.

While Charlie made the call, Edna watched John's retreating back with a mixture of thankfulness that he'd been there and annoyance at his chauvinism. Once he'd gone, leaving the side door open, she looked at the women still huddled together on the floor. Rosie was crying softly while Lily rocked her child back and forth, murmuring quietly.

When Charlie finished talking and closed his phone, she turned to him. "I must see about Lettie."

He put a restraining hand on her arm. "Better to wait. Help is on the way. You don't want Lettie to see her mother taken away in a police car, do you?"

Edna recognized the wisdom in his words and leaned back against the side of the Impala where Charlie joined her. They waited less than ten minutes before Detective Peggy King walked into the garage with two uniformed policemen. Before Edna knew it, Charlie was on his way to the station with Rosie and the officers, and Peggy King was escorting Lily into the house to release Lettie.

Edna headed home. She was uneasy. Something wasn't right.

Chapter 26

Weary as she was when she got home, Edna had a call to make.

"Hello, Irene."

"Edna? Hi. I was going to phone you later. Diane and I have been planning a surprise for the guys tomorrow night. Something special for Valentine's Day. I want to fill you in, but we have a couple more details to work out after she gets off work this afternoon."

"If you're thinking of a restaurant, it might be difficult to time a reservation. Their plane could be late."

"Oh, nothing like that. We're going to cook dinner at Diane's. Starling says she'll bring the appetizers." Irene giggled. "I bet she'll bring oysters from that favorite market of hers in Boston."

Edna smiled but didn't feel very festive at the moment. "Irene, I phoned to give you some bad news."

An edge of panic sounded in Irene's voice. "What's wrong? Nothing's happened to Matt, has it?" Before Edna could reply, Irene added, "Or Albert?"

"No, dear. The men are fine. I'm calling about Rosie Beck." Edna took a deep breath before continuing. "She's been arrested. It looks like she actually might have poisoned her husband two years ago. Nothing's definite yet, but they're questioning her."

"Oh, Edna, how terrible." After a second's pause,

Irene said, "How's Lettie? Is she okay?"

"She's with her grandmother and a policewoman. I'm not sure how she'll take the news of her mother, but I'll let you know as soon as I hear anything."

Irene was silent a while longer before she said, "What do I tell Amanda."

"Maybe you shouldn't say anything until we're certain."

"That's probably wisest," Irene agreed.

They ended the call shortly thereafter, promising to be back in touch if Edna received any information about the Becks, or if Irene had further details about the family dinner, although her enthusiasm for the event seemed to have diminished considerably.

Edna was restless for several hours after speaking to Irene. Something was nagging at her, but she couldn't bring it from the back of her mind into the light. Her thoughts switched from Lettie to Rosie, from Rosie to Lily, from Lily to Charlie, before starting again. Over and over, she wondered what they were doing, how they were feeling, and what was it that disturbed her about the whole affair. Wandering around the house, she half-heartedly straightened up for the cleaners who would arrive in the morning.

That evening, mostly to have something to do, she scrambled an egg and warmed a cranberry muffin. She had no appetite, but forced herself eat the light supper. She felt exhausted, but couldn't seem to sit still or lie down. She didn't want to go to bed or read, so she put on her coat and went for a walk.

The cold, humid air quickly seeped through her outer clothing and into her bones, but she didn't return to the house for another twenty minutes. The night was dark with only a partial moon, but the stars were bright in a clear sky. When she did finally open the door and enter the mudroom, the phone was ringing. Running through to the kitchen phone, she picked it up just as the answering machine kicked in.

"Hello, hello. I'm here," she nearly shouted into the receiver, hoping if it were either Albert or Charlie, he wouldn't have hung up.

When the "speak beep" sounded, Edna heard Charlie's voice.

"Where have you been? I've been trying to reach you for the past half hour."

"Walking. What's the news?"

"Nothing definite yet. Rosie's cooperating with us, but it's taking time to get things out of her. Also, she seems frantic about her daughter and keeps asking to see her."

"How is Lettie?"

"According to the children's advocate, she's clinging to Lily right now. Too soon to tell what will happen, but I'm guessing they'll leave the girl with her grandmother." Charlie paused and then added hesitantly, "I get the impression that Rosie isn't easy about her daughter staying with Lily."

"What makes you think that?" Edna was surprised at the comment, but upon hearing Charlie's comment, the fog in her head thinned slightly.

"Can't put my finger on it," He sighed. "Maybe I'm just tired and not thinking straight. Actually, I'm on my way home to get a few hours of shuteye before I go back."

Stalling for time in case her vague thoughts became clearer, she asked, "Have you seen John Forrester?"

"He stopped by the station just before I left."

"And?" Edna prompted. "Did he tell you why he was at Lily's and why he's been investigating a two-year-old case?" She hastened to add, "I'm very glad he was and I'm deliriously happy he went into that garage this morning, but I've never understood his motive."

"Said he was doing it for his daughter." Charlie clipped the last word off so abruptly, Edna knew he regretted saying it.

"Bobbi Callahan," she said, guessing John had asked Charlie to keep a confidence.

"You know about the relationship?" He sounded surprised.

"Yes," Edna said, "but only recently. I spoke to both Louise Callahan and Bobbi yesterday morning. It appears to be no secret, but neither do they want it to be the topic of gossip. The relationship is why he was taken off the case two years ago. According to his wife, Duke Callahan used his friendship with the chief to pull John from the investigation. Claimed it was a conflict of interest."

Charlie laughed. "I should have known you'd have the facts. Mary's influence, I imagine."

Edna ignored the remark as she spoke her next thought aloud. "So John decided to reinvestigate in order to protect his daughter." *Everyone seems to be protecting a daughter*, the voice in her mind said.

"So he claims," Charlie interrupted her musings. "Said everyone who was interviewed as a possible suspect two years ago has been living under a cloud of suspicion that won't be lifted until the truth comes out. Bobbi is afraid those doubts might jeopardize her teaching career. Folks might not want their kids associated with someone mixed up in an unsolved death. John told her he'd check, see if he could spot any stones left unturned. He told me that after reading the case file, he was pretty sure Rosie was responsible for her husband's death."

Not right, not right, the voice insisted. Straining to remove the remaining fuzziness from her brain, Edna said, "How did he come to be in Lily's garage this morning?"

"He wasn't getting anywhere with the case. He'd almost decided to give it up, but thought he'd question the Becks one more time, especially when he learned Rosie was at her mother's house. Figured he might learn something if the two women were together and he could get them pitted against each other."

Sounds like a tactic he'd use, Edna thought but didn't say aloud as Charlie went on speaking.

"When he drove by the place, he saw the garage door was partially open. Said he thought he might look around before announcing himself to the house. He told me, if nothing came of it, he'd probably have dropped the investigation."

Turning her mind to parents and children, Edna paid little attention to Charlie's last words. Perhaps it was a mother's instinct speaking when she said almost to herself, "Someone needs to interview Lettie."

"We'll be talking to her and to Lily," Charlie reassured Edna.

"No, I mean now." Edna hoped the sudden urgency

she felt was getting through to him. "Ask her about Saturday night."

"Oookaaay," Charlie drew out the single word.

"Trust me, Charlie. I think Lettie knows more than anyone suspects, including the child herself."

Chapter 27

Friday morning, after leaving instructions with the Housekeeper Helpers, Edna left for her weekly hair appointment and brunch with Peppa and Tuck. She wondered if Peppa would show up and if she had any more information about Clem. She did and she had, but the three friends could hardly shout across the room or speak while having their hair shampooed. For the first time that Edna could remember, Tuck waved off her usual root coloring. She didn't want to be late to the diner and miss any news.

Finally seated in their preferred booth in their favorite café with coffee and scones before them and the waitress gone, the three friends could talk.

Without preamble, Peppa said, "Peggy King came over last night."

Remembering that the lead detective had been a "Saturday morning kid" of Peppa's, Edna was certain Peggy made a special trip to give Peppa whatever information she could. Edna waited, trying to be patient, but questions whirled in her head.

"What did she say?" Tuck asked, sounding exasperated over the slowness at which her friend was imparting news. She watched Peppa intently as she bit into a blueberry scone and took a sip of coffee. "Don't tease," Tuck insisted. "Out with it, for heaven's sake."

Peppa swallowed, looking down into her coffee mug. Edna didn't think the old librarian was teasing. Rather, she was trying to get control of her emotions before speaking.

"Clem didn't take digitalis. What happened was he ate some sort of tainted honey that Lily had stored in her garage."

Edna nodded. "Mad honey."

"That's what Peggy said," Peppa agreed. "Charlie told her what you found in Mrs. Rabichek's journal and that it had properties similar to digitalis, suppressing his heart rate, besides making him disoriented and confused." She shook her head in sadness. "That, plus the physical strain and extreme cold, was enough to stop his heart altogether."

"Why did he eat the honey, if it wasn't any good?" Tuck demanded.

Peppa scowled at her. "He obviously didn't know what it was. Rosie told him he was welcome to anything he found in the garage cupboards. She said her mother tended to hoard her homemade goods, but Rosie thought the food would spoil, if it sat for too many years." Peppa took another bite of scone and chewed thoughtfully. "The police found a honey pot on Clem's kitchen table and figured he'd filled a honey pot from a pint of the bad stuff in the cupboard. They'll be testing it to make certain." Peppa sighed heavily. "Clem always had a sweet tooth, and he always preferred honey over sugar in his coffee, if you can imagine."

"How did he end up at your house?" Tuck asked, seeming too curious or excited to eat.

"Yes," said Edna, "and why was he holding a

Christmas Rose? Was he trying to point the finger at Rosie Beck?"

"Nobody knows," Peppa said. "I'm guessing he discovered how Gregory Haverstrum died and was taking a piece of the plant to show the police."

Tuck looked more confused than usual. "Why didn't he do that months ago?"

When Peppa merely shrugged, Edna spoke up. "I bet he recently found out the details of Gregory's death from John Forrester. The old detective has been talking to everyone associated with the case. Granted Clem wasn't around two years ago, but John's been hanging around Lily's place and would certainly have talked to Clem. As a botanist, Clem would have figured out that it must have been ranunculin that caused the blistering and ulcers around Gregory's mouth and in his throat. I think Peppa's right about Clem pulling the plant to show to the police."

The friends talked more, but their speculations soon petered out. Saddened by all that had happened in the last week, they cut short their visit and went to their respective homes.

For the rest of the day, Edna fidgeted as the clock moved slowly toward four-thirty when she would meet up with Charlie. Impatient for information, she wished he would phone before then with news of Lettie or Rosie, but wasn't surprised when he didn't. Edna was certain her hunch about the child was correct, that she had answers to questions nobody had thought to ask the youngster.

The hour finally came to leave. Edna was to drive to the police station and pick up Charlie before they headed for the airport to meet Albert, Matthew, Roger and Ken. To transport the men and their luggage, two cars were needed, so Starling had agreed to meet them at the baggage carousels.

When Edna reached the lot at the police station, she switched to the passenger's seat. Five minutes later, Charlie got behind the wheel and started the car. Edna didn't even wait for him to pull forward.

"Well," she said, "did you talk to Lettie?"

He put the car in gear and moved slowly out of the lot. "Peggy did. I told her you suggested asking Lettie what she did Saturday night." He glanced over at Edna. "You're pretty wily, you know that?"

Edna nearly bounced in the seat with nervous anticipation. "What did she say?"

Charlie watched for traffic as he accelerated onto the road. "Lettie said she and her mother were watching a movie. She said they were snuggled up on the couch in Lily's den 'cause it was a scary film. Her mother let her stay up late."

"Until what time?" Edna asked.

"Around eleven, according to the girl."

"So they must have been together when Clem was walking toward Peppa's house," Edna calculated.

"How did you know Lettie could alibi her mother?" Charlie gave Edna another quick glance.

"I didn't, but I remembered Lily saying she left halfway through the show. Innocent as children are, I doubt Lettie would consciously think to give her mother an alibi, if one were necessary."

Charlie nodded without taking his eyes off the road. "After talking to the girl, Peggy had Lily brought to the station for questioning. She resisted answering at first, but after Peggy told her about Lettie's confirmation of Rosie's alibi, Lily finally admitted to driving Clem away from her property. Said that on her way to bed, she'd gone to the sun porch to make sure the shades were drawn and spotted Clem stumbling around the back garden. Snow was falling pretty steadily by then, so she put on a coat and went to see what he was doing."

"And learned he had heard about Gregory Haverstrum's symptoms and connected them with the Christmas Rose," Edna finished for Charlie.

"Exactly." He glanced out the side view mirror before changing lanes and passing a slower vehicle. "Clem must have loaded his tea with the poisoned honey shortly before deciding to gather the evidence he'd need to prove his theory."

Edna shifted in her seat, turning slightly to study Charlie. "Rosie told me her mother never drove in bad weather. That's why I didn't suspect her sooner, but I still don't understand why Clem got into the car with her. He must have been leery of his employer. After all, it was her plant, her garden and her son-in-law."

"Remember, the 'mad honey' made him disoriented and weak. Lily probably had no problem getting him into Rosie's car, particularly if she told him she was taking him to the hospital."

"That's another thing. Why use Rosie's car? Was Lily trying to implicate her daughter?"

Charlie shook his head, keeping his eyes on the road. "She couldn't have used the Impala, even if she'd wanted to. Rosie was parked behind it in the driveway."

"Knowing her mother wouldn't have driven in the

snow," Edna completed the thought. She winced at the irony before asking, "Why did Lily leave Clem so close to his old house?"

"She didn't realize it was his old neighborhood. By that time, I'm guessing she wasn't thinking clearly. She admitted that all she could think about was getting him away from her place. Didn't care where and probably wasn't even aware of what street she was on. When she figured she'd driven around enough, she stopped, pushed him out of the car and drove off."

"Did she mean for him to die?"

"Claims not. She said she was 'terribly annoyed' at him for what she considered his disloyalty. She only wanted him away from her property. Like I said, she probably wasn't thinking rationally, but the forecast was for below-zero temperatures that night. I think she figured it was late enough at night and with the heavy snowfall, it was almost certain he wouldn't survive. Because of the condition he was in, she probably thought, if he did survive, he wouldn't remember what had happened."

"If you hadn't found out Rosie was with Lettie Saturday night, would Lily have let her daughter be blamed for Clem's death?"

"Her idea was that nobody could prove anything against Rosie, so she was waiting before implicating herself." Charlie looked over at Edna and raised his eyebrows, clearing doubting Lily's statement.

Edna shook her head at the mother's duplicity before speculating, "So Gregory Haverstrum was Lily's doing, too, I imagine. It certainly would explain Lettie's comment about her grandmother's medicine not making her father better. She must have seen Lily put something into her father's food or drink."

Charlie shrugged without glancing at Edna. "Probably, but we haven't pressed the girl about what she witnessed two years ago. For the time being, we've released Rosie." He slid his eyes toward Edna as if wondering how she would take the news, but before she could say anything about Rosie's manhandling of her, Charlie rushed on. "Her lawyer is taking responsibility for her staying in town, so Peggy thought it would be best if Rosie and Lettie could be together in Lily's house for the time being."

Realizing what Charlie's admission meant, Edna said, "I don't plan on pressing charges, but why did Rosie react as she did, threatening me with that pick?" Edna shuddered at the memory.

"Our department's psychologist spoke to her before Peggy agreed to release Rosie to her lawyer. She feels that John's reopening of the case stirred Rosie's subconscious. Her own repressed memories, plus questions Lettie'd begun to ask, pushed Rosie to the brink. She didn't want to believe her mother was capable of so heinous an act, and it put her psyche at odds with her growing conviction."

Edna was silent, thinking about all that had transpired in the last week until Charlie's voice brought her back to the present.

"Is there anything else about our case that you haven't figured out?" he said, flashing her a grin to let her know he was being facetious.

"Yes," she retorted, returning the smile. "How did you happen to walk into the garage when you did? That sort of timing only happens on TV shows."

He laughed. "Talk about a fluke. Lettie sent a text to Amanda. She was furious that her mother had locked her in her room, but she was also worried about her mother's strange behavior, so she sent a text to her best friend. Probably in the state Lettie was in, she forgot Amanda doesn't have a cell of her own and that the message would go to Starling's mobile. When she saw the message, Starling phoned me. Practically ordered me to get over to Lily's immediately." He gave Edna a lopsided grin. "Fortunately, my meeting was over."

Edna hid a smile, familiar with her daughter's bossy side, but not willing to acknowledge it to Charlie. Returning to the seriousness of the situation, Edna said, "Rosie's behavior certainly was strange." She shivered, remembering again the jab of the ice pick into her neck. "She took me completely by surprise, but that's another reason I thought she probably hadn't poisoned anyone."

Charlie frowned, sending another brief glance in Edna's direction. "Oh?"

"Poison is usually the weapon of a weak person. A coward, if you will," Edna explained. "Rosie went for me with a pick. If she had killed her husband, I imagine she would have used a knife or she would have hit him over the head with something. She was aggressive, not sly." Edna fell silent for a minute before voicing her next thought. "What do you suppose Lily's motive was in killing her son-in-law?"

Charlie shook his head. "I have no idea, but Peggy has a theory from what she learned during Rosie's interview. When she told her mother about the pending divorce and how unreasonable Gregory had become,

Lily decided to step in. Gregory threatened not only to get custody of Lettie, but also to make certain Rosie got practically no money from him. Lily was sure he could make good his threats, since Gregory had money to hire the best lawyers and Rosie had none. Even in his will, Haverstrum tied up all his assets in a trust for his daughter which she can't touch until she's twenty-five. Lily was in no position to help financially unless she sold the family home, so she did the only thing she could think of to protect her child. Lily had raised Rosie on a shoestring after her own husband died. She didn't want Rosie to go through the same struggle."

Edna sighed, feeling deeply saddened for the hopelessness Lily must have felt to have gone to such extremes. "What happens now?" she asked, thinking of the nine-year-old child who seemed caught in the middle.

Approaching the airport exit, Charlie put on his signal. "It's up to the lawyers," he said, turning off the highway.

When they reached the terminal, Charlie let Edna off at the arrivals door before driving off to park the car. She found Starling in the crowd waiting in the baggage claim area. Passengers were already coming off the escalators from the upper floor.

"I was wondering if you'd make it," Starling said, kissing her mother's cheek. "I thought I might have to squeeze four big men and their luggage into my little Toyota."

Charlie joined them as Edna finally spotted a familiar and beloved head of white, wavy hair. Instead of coming off the stairs, however, Albert and Matthew stepped out of an elevator. Roger and Ken were close behind. Her heart lurched when she saw her husband was still walking with the aid of his cane and his free hand was behind his back as if for balance. Smiling to hide her concern, she waved. Matthew saw her first and lifted a hand in acknowledgement.

As the men drew near, Albert suddenly swung out the arm that had been hidden and, with a slight bow, presented Edna with a prettily wrapped bouquet. He looked a little sheepish when he said, "I'm sorry, sweetheart, but the florist was completely sold out of roses."

"Thank goodness." The words slipped past her lips before she could stop them.

Behind her father, Starling had a sudden fit of coughing. As Charlie turned to pat her back, he caught Edna's eye and winked. She tried to ignore them both as she beamed up at her husband.

"Mums are perfect, dear."

#   #   #

Davies Family Recipes

With her busy schedule and four children to raise, Edna preferred quick, simple recipes that required few pans or dishes to wash. Here are some of her favorites that have become hits with her grandchildren, as well.

Chicken Pot Pie - Easy and Quick (serves 3 - 4)

    1 can (10.5 oz.) cream of potato soup
    10 oz. frozen mixed vegetables, partially thawed
    1 can (12.5 oz.) chicken breast, drained*
    1 egg, beaten
    1/2 cup milk
    1 cup baking mix

Preheat oven to 400 degrees.
In a 9 inch pie pan, combine soup, vegetables and chicken.
Beat egg in a small bowl. Add milk. Stir in baking mix until moist. Do not over stir. Mix should be lumpy, not smooth.
Pour baking mixture over chicken and vegetables.
Bake 25 minutes or until crust is nicely golden brown.

*Water may be reserved and given to cat in small doses, since it is too rich to be consumed at once.

Sweet and Sour Chicken - Slow Cooker (serves 2)

2 boneless, skinless chicken breasts (thawed or frozen)
1 small can (8 oz.) pineapple chunks with juice
1/2 cup Wishbone Russian salad dressing
1 green sweet bell pepper, seeded and cut into strips

Combine ingredients in slow cooker.
Pepper strips may be added during last hour of cooking, so as not to overcook.
If chicken is thawed, you may wish to cut breasts into 2 inch pieces.
Cook on low 6 to 8 hours or on high for 4 to 6 hours -- until chicken is thoroughly cooked. Frozen breasts will require the longer cooking times.
Serve over hot, cooked rice.

Breakfast Muffins - Cranberry
(makes 12 standard muffins)

> 2 cups flour
> 1/2 cup dried cranberries
> 1 tablespoon baking powder
> 2 tablespoons sugar
> 1/2 teaspoon salt
> 1 egg, beaten
> 1 cup milk
> 1/4 cup butter, melted

Preheat oven to 375 degrees.
Butter a 12-count muffin tin or use muffin papers.
In a large bowl, combine dry ingredients.
Stir in egg, milk and butter, but do not over stir. Batter should be lumpy, not smooth.
Fill muffin cups 2/3 full.
Bake 20 to 25 minutes or until center of a muffin will spring back to a poke.
Serve warm with lots more butter.

Popovers - Blender (makes 12)

     2 large eggs
     1 cup sifted flour
     1/4 teaspoon salt
     1 cup milk
     2 tablespoons melted butter

Preheat oven to 450 degrees.
Place muffin pan in oven to get very hot.
     (Do NOT use paper muffin cups for this recipe,
as Starling once did.)
Place all ingredients in blender and whirl until smooth.
Carefully grease hot muffin cups lightly w/ canola spray.
Fill muffin cups 1/2 full.
Bake for 15 minutes at 450. Lower heat and bake for
another 20 minutes at 375.
Serve hot with more butter.

Acknowledgements

I wish to thank Allen B. Gammons, Senior, for his fishing advice and for helping me to get rid of Albert this time--in the nicest possible way, of course.

To Mell McDonnell goes the credit for suggesting I add some of Edna's recipes to the back of this book. Thanks, Mell. Edna's pleased to share her family's favorites.

As always, I am indebted to Jan Reynolds, Jim Coleman, Gail Lindsey, Olivia Coleman and Lori Gee for their time, expertise and feedback as first readers.

I especially wish to acknowledge my critique partner Bonnie McCune (BonnieMcCune.com) who has stayed with me since 2000, generously sharing her support, guidance and insights. You're the best, Bonnie!

Last but certainly not least, heartfelt appreciation to my family, friends and readers who have been so supportive and encouraging. You make my efforts fun and rewarding.

About the Author

Suzanne Young was born and raised in Rhode Island. She has worked as a photographer, a writer, an editor, and a computer programmer and business analyst since earning her degree in English from the University of Rhode Island in Kingston.

A resident of Colorado for over 40 years, she retired from software development in 2010 to write fiction full time.

She is a member of Denver Woman's Press Club, Rocky Mountain Fiction Writers and Sisters in Crime as well as a graduate of the Arvada (CO) Citizens Police Academy.

To learn more about this author, she invites you to visit her website at http://suzanneyoungbooks.com/ where you can also contact her via e-mail.